Matt noticed a glow up ahead. If was as if the sun were trying to break through a thick fog.

"Sunshine!" he shouted as he struggled toward it through the snowbanks. "It's getting lighter. I know it's the sunshine!"

Suddenly he smacked against something hard enough to knock him backward. He lay in the snow, rubbing his aching nose and staring in disbelief. He could see the sunshine! It was just in front of him.

Cautiously he reached toward it. Something stoped his hand. Something invisible. Like a glass wall. Or a giant bubble.

Matt gasped. There was no way he could get out this time. He was trapped inside the blizzard.

Behind him, Bart was laughing like crazy.

Read these other BONE CHILLERS from HarperPaperbacks:

BONE CHILLERS

WELCOME TO ALIEN INN

BETSY HAYNES

HarperPaperbacks
A Division of HarperCollins*Publishers*

HarperPaperbacks   *A Division of* HarperCollins*Publishers*
                    10 East 53rd Street, New York, N.Y. 10022

Copyright © 1996 by Betsy Haynes and
Daniel Weiss Associates, Inc.

Cover art copyright © 1996 Daniel Weiss Associates, Inc.

First printing: January 1996

Printed in the United States of America

HarperPaperbacks and colophon are trademarks of
HarperCollins*Publishers*

❖ 10 9 8 7 6 5

For a super fan, Andrew Carroll,
who lives in Cincinnati, Ohio

Chapter

Lost! Little tingles of excitement traveled up Matt's spine when he heard his father say it.

It was a cold, blustery night on a winding backcountry road in the foothills of southern Vermont. The van belonging to twelve-year-old Matt Meyers and his family crept through hairpin curves. Its headlights probed the road ahead through the swirling snow and glanced off curtains of blue ice hanging from sheer walls of rock.

Matt's father sat hunched over the steering wheel, peering through the windshield as the wipers strained to clear away the accumulating slush. His mother sat rigidly erect at Mr. Meyers's side, her face drawn and tense.

Matt snuggled deeper into a blanket on the bench

1

seat behind his parents. Dotti, the family's Dalmatian dog, lay pressed against him, and his nine-year-old twin sisters, Ashlee and Julee, were asleep on the van's rear seat. The family was returning home to Fairfield, Connecticut, from their cabin near Mt. Snow, Vermont, after a fun-filled weekend of skiing. It was a trip they made almost every weekend in the winter, only this time something was different. Somehow they had gotten off their normal route. They were miserably, hopelessly lost.

"I don't understand where we made a wrong turn," Matt's mother said. "We've made this trip dozens of times."

"You're the navigator," Mr. Meyers answered tensely as he wiped away the moisture on the inside of the glass with a gloved hand. "I've got my hands full, keeping us out of a snowbank. Of all times to get lost. We've got to get home so that I can go to work tomorrow. I've got that big project going."

"And the children need to be in school," Matt's mother said anxiously.

"No, we don't," Matt piped up. "It won't hurt if we miss a day or two."

"Of course it will hurt if you miss a day or two," his mother said irritably. "You'll get behind, and catching up is never easy."

"Well, I know *I* won't get behind," Matt grumbled.

2

"How could I? School's totally boring, and we never learn anything interesting."

"Matt! Stop arguing with your mother," his father said sternly.

Matt sighed and rolled his head against the window, looking out into the darkness. He knew better than to argue with his father, especially when he was upset, like he was now. Instead Matt watched in fascination as huge snowflakes, the size of miniature snowballs, splatted against the glass. He had never seen it snow so hard. Suddenly a gust of wind buffeted the van, and Dotti snuggled closer.

Matt's imagination went into high gear. What if the van rolled into a deep ravine, and he and his family had to hole up in a cave? They would have to build a fire and live off melted snow and whatever leftover food was still in the cooler from the weekend. And what if search teams braved the blizzard to comb the countryside looking for them?

Wow! he thought. Then he would really have something cool to tell his friends about when he got back to school.

His mother shot to attention. "What's that up ahead?" she asked, leaning forward and pointing. "Are those lights?"

Mr. Meyers swiped at the windshield again and looked into the darkness. "Maybe . . ."

3

Matt leaned forward and squinted to see past the glow of the dash lights. He saw something, too. The dark shape of a roof appeared among the trees. Then, as they got closer, he could see walls and softly lit windows. Quickly the shadow became a two-story chalet-type building. The windows were aglow like beacons in the night.

At first he was disappointed to see something as ordinary as a building that looked like a ski lodge. Then he looked closer and did a double take.

"Look at the sign out front," cried Matt. "It says SNOWED INN. Hey, that's cool!"

"Well, it's certainly appropriately named," said his mother with a nervous laugh. "I hope they have some vacant rooms."

"There aren't any other cars in the parking lot, so maybe we're in luck," said Mr. Meyers. "But they may be expecting people soon. It looks as if the lot has just been plowed."

He maneuvered the van into a space near the front door and pulled to a stop.

"Are we home?" came a sleepy voice from the back of the van.

"No, Ashlee. We're lost in a snowstorm, and we're stopping at a lovely old inn for the night," said her mother.

"Gosh, do you think they'll let Dotti come in?"

4

asked Matt. He slipped a protective arm around the dog and stroked her head.

"I'm sure they will, dear," his mother replied. "No one would be cruel enough to make a poor dog stay outside on a night like this."

As if to underscore her words, a huge gust of wind rocked the van, slapping a wall of snow against it.

"Hurry, kids. Let's get inside," urged Mr. Meyers.

Matt snapped the leash on Dotti as they scrambled out of the van and into the snowstorm. He could barely stand up against the force of the wind.

"It's getting worse, girl," he muttered to Dotti.

Dotti pricked her ears, pointed her nose up, and sniffed wildly at the wind. Then she tugged on the leash, backing toward the van again.

"What's the matter, Dotti?" Matt said, pulling her toward the door of the inn. "Believe me, you don't want to stay out here."

It took a couple of hard pulls on the leash for Matt to get her going. His parents herded him and his sisters and Dotti up the stairs and onto a large veranda.

When Mr. Meyers opened the double doors and the family stepped inside, they were greeted with delicious warmth coming from a flickering fire in a huge stone fireplace directly across the lobby of the beautiful lodge. Large oak-beams ran the length of the ceiling, and hand-crocheted rugs dotted the gleaming hardwood floors. Lined up in front of the fireplace was a row of overstuffed sofas and chairs, most of them draped with cozy afghans.

A man and a woman, who were about the age of Matt's grandparents, were the only people in the room. They were sitting together on a sofa near the registration desk. When Matt and his family approached the desk, they looked up and smiled and began to whisper to each other, their faces glowing red in the soft firelight.

Matt started to smile back, but he blinked and looked again. Was he seeing things? All of the furniture and the two people sitting on the sofa were turned with their backs to the fire!

"Weird," he mumbled under his breath.

He noticed that his mother was looking at the strange arrangement, too. But just as he started to say something to her, he glanced toward the game room and noticed three children inside, playing games on the electronic machines. He squinted at them. There was a boy about his age and two girls. One of the girls was about Ashlee and Julee's age, but the other was much younger. The boy's hair was lighter than Matt's and cut short. The two girls had sandy-blond hair. The two older kids looked like they were having a great time playing the games, while the smaller girl watched.

6

The man sitting on the sofa stood up and started toward them.

"Welcome to Snowed Inn. Welcome to all of you and your lovely dog, too. May I help you?" he asked, smiling kindly.

Matt thought the man looked familiar, but he couldn't remember where he had seen him before. He was thin and dressed neatly in slacks and a cardigan sweater.

"We're the Meyers," said Matt's father, rushing forward and extending his hand. "We're lost and need a place to stay for the night. I've got to get home tomorrow so that I can get to work. I sure hope you've got a vacancy."

The man looked at Mr. Meyers's hand in surprise for a moment and then reached out and gingerly touched the palm with his finger.

"Rogers is my name. *Mr.* Rogers," he said, chuckling. "We've got just the room for a nice-looking family like you. Welcome to my neighborhood."

Matt's mouth fell open as he stared at Mr. Rogers. Now he knew where he had seen the man before. On television in the children's program where he always said exactly the same thing: "Welcome to my neighborhood."

Matt blinked at the man. This was *too* weird. Where were they, anyway? At his feet, Dotti let out a low growl.

Chapter 2

Mr. Rogers stepped behind the desk and opened the registration book, looking expectantly at Matt's father.

Mr. Meyers glanced around the desktop and then asked, "Um . . . do you have a pen?"

The desk clerk seemed confused and looked at the woman whom Matt assumed was his wife.

"In the upper right-hand drawer, dear," said the small, gray-haired woman, nodding toward the desk.

Matt glanced around the room. Things were getting stranger by the minute. If Mr. Rogers was the regular desk clerk at Snowed Inn, wouldn't he know where to find a pen? Now his wife was leaning forward in her seat, watching. It was as if he were about to perform brain surgery or do something equally fascinating. Even the three kids in the game room had stopped playing and were standing in the doorway, staring at Matt and his family. It made Matt's skin crawl.

Mr. Rogers fumbled through the drawer and pulled out a pair of scissors, handing it to Mr. Meyers.

Matt's dad started to reach for it, then seeing that it was a pair of scissors instead of a pen, he dropped his hand and looked at Mr. Rogers with a puzzled expression.

"No, no," the gray-haired woman said quickly. She frowned and pointed to the drawer again.

Looking embarrassed, Mr. Rogers put back the scissors and pulled out a ruler. He didn't hand it to Matt's father this time. Instead he looked questioningly at his wife again. She shook her head impatiently. Finally he picked up a ballpoint pen, and she nodded. "Thank you, dear," he murmured.

"Here you are, sir," said Mr. Rogers, handing the pen to Matt's father.

Mr. Meyers shook his head in amazement and took it. Matt watched nervously as his father signed the register. Why wouldn't anybody know the difference between a pen and scissors or a ruler?

"Dad," he whispered urgently, tugging on the sleeve of his father's ski jacket. "Let's not stay here. This place is creepy."

Mr. Meyers gave him an annoyed frown. "Hush, Matt. We don't have any choice. There's a blizzard going on out there."

"I don't want to go out in the snow again," wailed Julee.

"Me either," said Ashlee.

Their father had turned back to Mr. Rogers. "How much are the rooms?" he asked. He pulled a credit card out of his wallet, which he held out for the clerk to take.

"Reasonable," Mr. Rogers assured him. He shook his head and pushed the credit card away. "Don't worry the least bit about that until you check out. Matter of fact, we've got a special on two connecting rooms, which should be just perfect for your family."

"Great," said Mr. Meyers. "I'm really beat and I have a pounding headache. A hot shower and a soft bed sound wonderful. Come on, kids. Let's bring in the luggage."

Matt glanced at the registration book as he moved away from the desk. Their family's name was the only entry on the page.

That's really weird, he thought, shaking his head. *What about the kids in the game room? Are they Mr. and Mrs. Rogers's children?*

Matt trudged after his dad and two sisters. When

the front door opened, a blast of icy air almost knocked him off his feet, and sleet stung his face. His father had been right. They couldn't go back out on the road. Weird or not, they'd have to stay at Snowed Inn for the night.

They unloaded everything from the van except the skis, which were frozen in the rack on top of the car, and hauled it all back into the lobby of the inn. Mrs. Meyers waited there with Dotti.

"Mr. Rogers said our rooms are upstairs, the third and fourth doors on the right," she said. "I have the keys."

She led the way upstairs. Dotti slunk along beside her, looking around nervously. The girls and Mr. Meyers followed. Matt brought up the rear, lugging a canvas bag full of ski boots. He still had a creepy feeling about the place.

At the top of the stairs he turned and looked back down at the lobby. Mr. and Mrs. Rogers and the three children were standing at the foot of the stairs, staring up at him. As if on cue, they all smiled in unison.

Matt whirled around and raced after the others. "Wait up," he said nervously.

He could hear Julee and Ashlee laughing even before he entered the room where the twins were bouncing up and down on a big feather bed. It was so tall that they'd had to climb up on a little stool to get on. Dotti was cowering in the corner, and Matt thought for an instant that he could see her teeth chattering.

"Come on, Matt! This is fun!" Ashlee called out.

Matt slung the bag of ski boots on his own bed and vaulted onto it. "Forget it," he said, stretching out on the soft bed. But he immediately discovered that his feet were higher than his head. Sitting up again, he did a double take. The pillows were at the foot of the bed instead of at the head.

"Children! Children!" said Mrs. Meyers. She was standing in the doorway to the adjoining room, shaking her head. "Shhhh. You're going to disturb the other guests," She dropped to one knee beside Dotti and stroked her head to calm her.

"If there *are* any other guests," muttered Matt. "I can't understand why no one else is here."

A shadow crossed his mother's face. "I'll have to admit, things are a little unusual here," she said. "I'll be glad when the snow stops and we can be on our way."

"Let's go down to the game room," said Julee, a few minutes later. "I'm tired of bouncing on this bed, and I want to meet those other kids."

"Me too," said Ashlee. "And the electronic games looked cool."

"Matt, are you coming?" asked Julee. She was already heading for the door.

Matt hesitated for a moment. "I guess so," he said, hopping down from the bed and following his sisters.

He just hoped the kids weren't as weird as everything else in this place.

Chapter

3

"**L**ook! The kids are still in the game room," Julee said excitedly when they were back downstairs. She pointed toward the dark room where Matt could see the three children standing in front of video screens that pulsed and glowed in every color.

"Hi, come on in," called the boy.

Matt hesitated. The boy looked okay. Matt knew he was probably just spooked by the emptiness of Snowed Inn. He was being silly.

Julee and Ashlee were already in the game room talking to the girls when Matt stepped inside.

"Hi, I'm Lisa," he heard one of them say to the twins.

"And I'm Maggie," said the other.

"My name's Bart," said the boy, walking up to Matt.

"Bart? And they're Lisa and Maggie?" Matt asked in surprise. "That's wild. You guys have the same name as the kids on *The Simpsons*."

Bart grinned. "Yeah. Cool, isn't it? Want to play some games?"

Matt brightened up immediately as he looked around. "Sure," he said. "I'm Matt, Matt Meyers. This place has some cool games."

His eyes roamed over the electronic machines, scanning the titles. In Search of the Burrowing Altairians. Battling the M42 Plyomith Warrior. To one side were booths players could sit in or stand in to play Solar Windsurfing and Black-Hole Diving into Cygnus X-1.

"Wow! We don't have any of these back home," Matt said excitedly. He stepped up to Battling the M42 Plyomith Warrior and pulled a quarter out of his pocket. "Where's the coin slot?"

"You don't need any money," said Bart. "They're all free. All you have to do is push that button on the front."

Matt stepped up to the booth and poked at the button. Orange and blue lights flashed on, and the room was filled with loud, eerie music that sounded to Matt more like a pair of cats fighting than like any music he'd ever heard before.

Suddenly, out of nowhere, an evil-looking man dressed in tight-fitting futuristic clothes loomed menacingly over Matt. His glowing eyes held Matt's like twin sword-points.

Matt jumped back in alarm. Behind him, Julee and Ashlee shrieked.

"You have dared to challenge a Plyomith warrior, Earthling," the man said in a deep, gravelly voice that sounded like Darth Vadar and echoed off the walls of the room. "Choose your weapon!"

Matt stared at him with an open mouth and backed toward the door. This wasn't a video game!

"He's not real," Bart said, and laughed. "He's a hologram of a warrior from the planet Plyomith."

Lisa giggled. "Yeah, just push the start button when you're ready to fight him," she said.

"Wow!" said Matt. He glanced at the hologram again and sucked in his breath. He looked so real! Matt stepped forward and pushed the button. "This is *really cool*."

Pictures of six futuristic-looking weapons appeared on the screen next to the warrior.

"Point to the weapon you want," Bart said.

Matt looked them over carefully. One was triangular with a pair of pointed antennae sticking out the longest tip. Another was round with blinking lights. Matt pointed to one that looked more like a

16

TV remote control than a weapon. Suddenly it appeared in his hand.

"It's not real, either," Bart assured him. "It just feels that way."

Matt pulled his hand nearer and looked at the quavering image of his weapon. But how was he supposed to use it? What would happen if he pushed one of the buttons?

Without warning, the Plyomith warrior grabbed an identical weapon from his belt and pointed it toward Matt.

"Cowabunga! Shoot!" cried Matt.

Matt pointed the gun at the hologram, but a blast of light from the Plyomith warrior's weapon hit him squarely in the chest.

"Ouch!" he yelped. He looked down and rubbed the spot, but strangely there was no hole.

"You're dead! You're dead!" shouted Maggie.

"That's okay. Nobody ever beats a Plyomith warrior," said Lisa sympathetically.

"But I wasn't ready," complained Matt. "It wasn't fair. I didn't even know how to play this stupid game. I want to try again."

"Go ahead," said Bart, giving him a knowing grin.

Matt stepped up to the game again. This time he chose a wicked-looking weapon with three razor-sharp prongs. But the hologram surprised him from behind, and he lost again. The next time Matt was dead before he could figure out how to hold his weapon. Finally he turned away in disgust.

"It isn't any fun if you don't even have a chance," he muttered.

"Try Solar Windsurfing," suggested Bart. "Maybe you can do that one."

Matt gave Bart a skeptical look.

"Go ahead. Try it," urged Ashlee.

"I dare you," said Julee.

Matt couldn't resist a dare, so he stepped into the booth and pushed a button on the wall. Instantly he was wearing a suit that resembled the wet suits scuba divers wear. Even more amazing, he was standing on a surfboard somewhere in outer space!

Huge, unseen winds began buffeting him. He ducked and rolled, fighting to keep his balance, but the winds grew stronger, and the board rocked and bobbed like a tiny cork in wild seas. He felt himself falling. The next thing he knew, he had tumbled out of the booth and was sprawled on the game-room floor.

The other kids were all laughing.

"Wow, you didn't last long at that one, either," said Julee.

Embarrassed, Matt got up and brushed himself off. "Let's see you try it," he grumbled.

18

"Don't feel bad," said Bart. "It took me a while to learn to play these games. You practice every day, and you'll catch on."

"We won't be here that long," said Matt, sighing. "We have to leave in the morning. My dad has to get to work, and we have to get to school."

Bart got a strange look on his face. Staring deep into Matt's eyes, he said slowly, "You may be here a lot longer than you think."

"What are you talking about?" demanded Matt. He didn't like the way Bart had said that. It sounded almost as if he knew something Matt didn't know.

Bart shrugged. His strange expression had disappeared. "What I meant was, you never know how long these snowstorms will last."

Matt stared at Bart. Suddenly he didn't feel like playing video games anymore. And he didn't feel like hanging around Bart any longer, either.

"Come on, girls," he said, motioning to the twins. "It's getting late. We'd better get back to our room before Mom and Dad start looking for us."

"We don't want to go yet," whined Ashlee. "We're having fun."

"Yeah, and we just met Bart and Lisa and Maggie," said Julee, looking at him with pleading eyes.

"I said, come on!" Matt ordered.

He headed for the stairs without looking back.

Chapter

"Don't go upstairs yet, okay?"

Matt blinked in surprise. To his astonishment, Bart was standing at the bottom of the staircase in front of him—if it really was Bart. He looked different, but Matt couldn't put his finger on why. Lisa and Maggie were on either side of Bart, and they looked different, too. At least Maggie did. She looked bigger. Almost as tall as Lisa.

How had Bart and the girls gotten past him and made it to the stairs without his seeing them? he wondered, shaking his head.

"It's not that late," Bart insisted. "We could sit in here by the fireplace and talk."

"Yeah, I'm dying to hear about your school," said Lisa, turning to Julee and Ashlee.

"Do you guys have boyfriends?" Maggie asked excitedly.

"We don't have to go up yet, do we, Matt?" begged Julee.

"Mom and Dad won't care if we stay down here a little while longer. Please, Matt, can't we stay?" Ashlee asked, looking at him with pleading eyes.

Matt glanced at the big smile on Bart's face. Maybe he'd been imagining things again. The funny feeling he'd had when Bart said they might be here longer than they thought was probably silly. Bart had just been making conversation. And the impression he had that Bart and Maggie looked different was probably his imagination, too. After all, a lot had happened that day. He'd gone from skiing to getting lost in a snowstorm to being snowed in at a ski lodge called, crazily enough, Snowed Inn.

"Okay," Matt said. "Grab the other end of this sofa, Bart, and let's turn it around the way it's supposed to be. I don't know who arranged the furniture in here, but they sure have a weird sense of humor."

Bart hurried to help turn the sofa around while Ashlee and Julee each turned a chair toward the fireplace and sat down. Lisa and Maggie did the same.

"Hey, Matt. What do you do for fun?" asked Bart when everyone was settled.

Matt shrugged. "The usual, I guess. Mostly hang out at the mall with my friends. Go swimming at Fairfield beach in the summer. Play ball and video games."

"What's a mall?" asked Lisa.

Both Julee and Ashlee's mouths dropped open in amazement.

"You don't know what a *mall* is?" gasped Ashlee. "I couldn't *live* without going to the mall."

"Um . . . we live in a small town," said Maggie, looking embarrassed.

"Wow. It must be awfully small and way out in the boonies if you don't know what a mall is," said Julee. "I mean, *really!*"

"A mall," Ashlee began patiently, "is . . . well, it's a bunch of stores that are all in one building. And there's usually a food court where you can buy stuff like pizza, burgers and fries, tacos, things like that."

"All the kids we know hang out at the mall," Julee added.

"Unless they're at the beach," said Matt.

"Is the beach another kind of mall?" asked Bart.

"Not funny," said Matt. "You're putting me on." Matt glared at Bart. The guy was too much.

"I'm not trying to be funny, or putting you on," Bart argued, saying the last three words as if they didn't quite fit his mouth. "And I remember now. A beach is a place with all that sand. We don't have a beach where we live. Like my sister said, we're from a really, *really* small town. We don't go many places, and our parents won't let us watch much TV."

"So what are you doing here if you don't *ever* go anywhere?" Matt asked.

Bart's face was blank for an instant. Then a smile broke across it. "Over the river and through the woods, to Grandmother's house we go," he said proudly. "That's where we're going. To Grandmother's house."

"So where does your grandmother live?" Matt asked, even though he didn't really care.

"Live?" Bart asked in surprise. "Oh, well, she . . . uh . . . we're already there. She lives *here*. She's Mrs. Rogers, and Mr. Rogers is our grandfather," he said proudly.

Matt stared into the crackling fire, not knowing exactly what to make of Bart. In a way, he felt sorry for him. *If* he was telling the truth. But how could anyone be from such a small town that they didn't know anything about what went on in the world? Everybody knew what a mall was. And a beach. But not good old Bart. And the girls were just as dumb.

"Tell us about your house," said Lisa. "Is it as big as this house?"

"No, silly," said Ashlee. "It's just a regular-size house with three bedrooms. This place is *huge*."

"Is it in California with a big swimming pool?" asked Maggie, her eyes sparkling.

Julee shook her head and looked annoyed. "Of course not. California is three thousand miles away. What's the matter with you, anyway? Don't you have geography in school?"

Suddenly Matt realized that Bart and his sisters' grandparents had come into the room. They were tiptoeing closer and closer, as if they were trying to eavesdrop on the children's conversation.

He stood up abruptly. "Come on, Julee. Come on, Ashlee. We'd better go now."

"We'll see you in the morning, won't we?" asked Lisa.

"Sure," murmured Matt.

But deep down he hoped more than anything in the world that the snow would stop during the night, and in the morning they'd be *out of there!*

Chapter

When Matt's eyes popped open the next morning, he didn't know where he was. Then he caught sight of Julee and Ashlee sleeping in the bed across the room, and it all came back to him. He was snowed in at Snowed Inn.

Rolling over, he pressed his nose against the windowpane and looked out. It was still snowing. Harder than ever. Drifts as high as his head were piled up against the building, and the wind was howling like a hurt animal.

"Rats!" he muttered, and pulled the covers back over his head. His family wouldn't be leaving for home anytime soon.

He had felt Dotti leap onto his bed and crawl under the covers sometime during the night. Now she snuggled closer. It gave him a cozy feeling to have her so near and he snuggled back, deciding to stay under the warm covers a little while longer.

He had almost drifted off to sleep again when he heard a humming noise start up. It was so faint that he had to strain to hear it, but it was there, all right. Touching the wall, he felt a slight vibration.

Must be the heating system, he thought, remembering the funny noises the steam furnace made at home.

The next thing he knew, he was waking up again. His mother was beside the bed, shaking him gently.

"Wake up, sleepyhead," she said. "Your dad and I and the twins have been up for ages. We're all hungry as bears. Get your clothes on so we can go down for breakfast."

Matt climbed slowly out of his warm bed. The room was chilly, and he grabbed the shirt that he'd pitched over a chair the night before, and the pants from where he'd hung them on the bedpost, and hurriedly put them on.

Mr. Rogers met them at the entrance of the dining room a few minutes later, carrying a handful of menus. "Welcome to my neighborhood," he said cheerfully. "Come right this way."

To Matt's amazement, people were seated at half a dozen tables.

He tapped his father on the shoulder. "Where did *they* come from?" he asked.

His dad shrugged. "Must have checked in during the night."

Everyone seated at the tables they passed looked up and nodded pleasantly. Mr. Rogers pulled out a chair for Matt's mother and handed each of them a menu.

"Someone will be right with you," he said.

"Look, Ashlee. There are Lisa and Maggie over by the window," Julee said.

Matt glanced in the direction Julee pointed. Bart was there, too, and he waved at Matt.

Matt groaned inwardly. He wasn't sure he could take much more of Bart.

"It's funny that the inn is so full. I didn't see any cars in the parking lot when we went through the lobby," Mr. Meyers said, shaking his head.

"Maybe there's an underground parking garage that Mr. Rogers forgot to tell us about," suggested Ashlee.

"Or maybe all these people belong to one of those ski clubs that rent a bus to bring them to ski areas," said Julee. "It'll probably be back later to pick them up."

Matt glanced around the room. Most of the people didn't look like skiers. They looked like business people or retired schoolteachers. And some

27

of them were wearing funny-looking clothes that looked like those he'd seen in old-fashioned movies.

Suddenly Julee burst out giggling. "Look at that!" she said, pointing to her menu. "Breakfast is spelled *Brekfus!*"

Matt looked down at his menu and did a double take. Julee hadn't been kidding.

I imagine it's just another way of being quaint," said his mother, chuckling softly.

Mr. Meyers nodded. "It reminds me of that Italian restaurant we ate at in Greenwich Village named Busghetti's instead of Spaghetti's."

"Look how they spell pancakes," said Matt, pointing down the page. *"Pan Kaks."*

"And waffles is spelled *Wah Fulls,"* said Julee, giggling again.

"If you want my opinion, thay're carrying quaintness a little far," said their father. "And, boy! Does Mr. Rogers ask a lot of questions. I went downstairs looking for a newspaper last night while you children were in the game room, and he began giving me the third degree. He wanted to know all sorts of things about the kind of work I do and the house we live in. You'd think he was born on another planet."

"I had the same experience with his wife when I went looking for a laundry room," Mrs. Meyers said, shaking her head. Then she chuckled and added, "She even wanted to know if my detergent was ninety-nine and forty-four one-hundredths percent pure. I hadn't heard that since I was a child and used to hear Ivory Soap commercials on the radio."

"There are a lot of things that are strange around here," Matt said. "Bart and his sisters give me the creeps with all their questions."

"Me too," said Ashlee. "They ask the dumbest things."

"Yeah, but who else are we going to play with?" Julee asked glumly. "They're the only other kids here."

"May I take your order now?" asked a waitress who seemed to appear out of nowhere.

"Oh, uh, yes," said Mr. Meyers, looking up in surprise.

When they had all placed their orders, Matt's dad pushed his chair away from the table and stood up before Matt could start the conversation again about how strange things were.

"I think I'll check at the front desk and see if they've heard a weather report," said Mr. Meyers. "Surely this storm won't last much longer. We have to get on the road again."

Matt watched his father leave the dining room, thinking that there wasn't much use talking about all the strange things going on around Snowed Inn, anyway. They'd be gone before he knew it. And besides, maybe he just had cabin fever and thought things were stranger than they really were.

He looked up when he saw his father returning to the table, a deep frown creasing his forehead.

"I just heard the radio report myself," he said. "There's a huge blizzard blanketing the whole East Coast. They don't know when it will blow through. Looks like we're stuck here at least until tomorrow."

"Rats," said Julee. "I guess we'll have to put up with a million more questions from Lisa and Maggie all day."

Matt scowled at the thought of being stuck at Snowed Inn and having to talk to Bart. He remembered how excited he had been at the idea of being snowed in and missing school. He had thought it would be a big adventure. Boy, had he been wrong.

Just then the waitress came bustling up to the table, balancing a tray of food over her head.

Matt hadn't realized how hungry he was until he smelled the delicious aroma of bacon and eggs. His mouth started watering like a broken fire hydrant as the waitress set a plate in front of him.

He looked into the plate and blinked twice. He had ordered bacon, eggs, and a short stack of pancakes. What he had gotten was four hard-cooked fried eggs—stacked one on top of the other.

"I didn't order any *meat*," Ashlee said indignantly. "And look. All I have is three strips of bacon and a slice of ham!"

"Well, at least that's better than what I got," said Julee. She was staring down at an omelette sandwiched between two waffles with whipped cream and a cherry on top.

If this doesn't convince them that everybody in this place is crazy, nothing will, thought Matt. He looked across the table to see that his father had a poached egg floating in a bowl of soggy cereal, and his mother had two eggs with a waffle on top. To make matters worse, their parents had milk served in coffee cups, and each of the children had coffee in drinking glasses.

The family looked from one to another in amazement.

"Where's the waitress?" their mother asked, looking around the dining room. "She made a mistake on all the orders."

But the waitress had disappeared.

Then Mr. Meyers chuckled softly. "You know, I think they mixed up our orders on purpose. It must be the way they initiate new guests to make them feel at home. I certainly hope so, anyway."

He turned to an elderly couple at the next table and laughed, pointing to his food. "Pretty funny, right?" he asked.

The couple laughed, too. Matt turned around and saw that everyone in the whole room was laughing.

"See, what'd I tell you?" said his father, looking relieved. "It's a kind of initiation for first-time guests."

Matt couldn't believe how his parents were taking this. He knew they had always taught him and his sisters to make the best of a bad situation, but this was unreal! Was he the only one who could see that something strange was going on?

"If you ask me, it's weird," he mumbled, and stuck a fork into his stack of eggs.

Chapter

Matt's eggs tasted terrible. He loaded them with salt, but it didn't help. Plastic would have been more tasty.

No one else at the table was eating with enthusiasm, either.

"These waffles taste like Styrofoam," complained Julee. "They need to get a better cook in this place."

Again, the waitress seemed to materialize out of thin air.

"Is everything okay?" she asked.

"I'm afraid you got our orders mixed up," said Mrs. Meyers. "And the menu . . . everything is misspelled."

"Oh, that," said the waitress, pointing to a menu in her hand. "We made up the menu that way on purpose as a challenge to the children. Actually it's a game. We like to see which child can find all the errors and correct them the fastest."

She reached into her pocket and pulled out three pencils, handing one to Matt and the others to Julee and Ashlee. "Here's a pencil for each of you to write in your corrections," she went on. "The one who corrects all the menu items first wins a scrumptious dessert. Your parents will judge if you've found all the mistakes. That makes it a family game."

"What a nice idea," commented Mrs. Meyer.

"I like it better when there's a place mat you can color," grumbled Ashlee. "This is no fun."

"Go ahead, children," urged their father. "It will help you with your spelling."

Julee and Ashlee reluctantly picked up their pencils, but Matt shoved his aside. "It's a baby game," he muttered. But that wasn't all that bothered him about it. He suspected that the people at Snowed Inn didn't know how to spell the things on the menu any more than they knew how to fix the dishes.

Suddenly he noticed two men enter the dining room dressed in football uniforms.

"Look at those guys," he said in amazement. "They've got on pads and helmets and everything."

The two men were wearing black uniform pants

and orange jerseys with numbers on them, but no team name. Their faces were hard to see because of the face masks on the fronts of the helmets, but it was easy to hear them coming. They were wearing cleats!

"Are they going to a costume party?" his mother asked the waitress.

"Oh, no, ma'am. They're going to the Super Bowl," she announced proudly.

Mrs. Meyers looked at the others at the table and frowned. "Isn't it a little odd to wear uniforms to a restaurant?" she asked.

"I think it's cool," said Julee.

"It's not cool," argued Matt. "And besides, they couldn't be going to the Super Bowl. It was played two weeks ago."

"You're right, son," said his father. "That is strange, isn't it?" He glanced toward the two football players, frowning, and shook his head.

"May I be excused?" Matt asked. He didn't want to stay in the dining room any longer.

"But you haven't finished your breakfast," said his mother.

"I'm not hungry, and even if I was, these eggs are awful," Matt said. He saw a frown forming on his mother's face and added, "And I want to take Dotti out. She hasn't been out since last night."

"Good idea, son," Mr. Meyers said.

Matt scooted out of the dining room before his mother could protest. It felt good to escape that place. He hurried up the stairs, eager to see Dotti.

"She's the only sane one here," he muttered under his breath.

He unlocked the door to the room he shared with his sisters and went inside, but he didn't see Dotti anywhere. The maid had cleaned the room and made the beds. He stood in the middle of the room and looked around. Dotti wasn't on either of the beds. She wasn't stretched out on the floor. Where could she be?

"Dotti? Dotti, come here, girl," he called softly. He poked his head into the bathroom, but she wasn't there, either. He looked under the beds. No Dotti. And she wasn't in the adjoining bedroom his parents shared.

"Oh, I know. Dumb me! I should have figured it out before," he said to himself. "The maid must have left the door open while she was cleaning, and Dotti went exploring."

He hurried back into the hall and looked in both directions. No Dotti. He started toward the stairway leading to the lobby and changed his mind. *I might as well look up here first*, he thought.

He wandered up the dark and gloomy hallway,

stopping at every door to see if it was open and if the dog had wandered inside.

"Dotti, Dotti! Where are you?" he called. "Wanna go outside, girl?"

By the time he had been to the end of the hall and back, Matt was convinced that Dotti wasn't upstairs. He made a quick stop in his room again to get her leash and a handful of dog treats and headed downstairs.

The lobby was deserted, and a radio he hadn't noticed before crackled with static on the registration desk.

"And now for the latest weather," an announcer said through the static. "According to the National Weather Service, a large blizzard is blanketing the East Coast. Meteorologists say a high pressure system is stalled and is blocking the cold front, and it could be several days before it moves out into the Atlantic Ocean."

"Several days!" Matt cried in disbelief. "They've got to be kidding!"

He stuffed his fists into his jeans pockets and went over to warm himself before the fire. He needed to find Dotti and take her outside. It was going to be miserable out there, and he had left his coat up in the room.

Matt glanced around at all the sofas and chairs to

see if she was snuggled up in one of them. No luck. Then he looked toward the dining room. She wouldn't be in there. Not that she wouldn't want to be, he thought, but he knew a begging dog in a restaurant would be kicked out fast.

Glancing past the game room, he saw a hallway that angled off to the left and appeared to be narrow and dark.

It didn't make sense that she would go down a dark, narrow hallway, but he headed toward it anyway. There was no place else to look.

The hall was shorter than the one upstairs, with two doors on either side and a double door at the end. The sound of his footsteps was muted by thick carpeting.

It only took a second to realize Dotti wasn't in the hall. There was nothing for her to hide behind, and all the doors were closed.

Still, Matt reasoned, maybe one of them had been left open earlier, and Dotti had wandered inside. Cautiously he tried the first door on the right. It was locked. So was the first door on the left. He tried the next door on the left side of the hall. It was locked, too.

This is a waste of time, he thought, and turned to go back to the lobby.

He stopped. Had he heard a funny sound coming

from the room at the end of the hall? The one with the double doors?

Pressing an ear against the door, he listened again. There were voices! But they were speaking in a high-pitched tone and in a language he had never heard before. They sounded more mechanical than human, like a tape recording being played backward. But there were two of them, and they were definitely carrying on some kind of conversation. One voice sounded young and excited. The other, older and more cautious.

"Ugeeh lsier vbk! Wqqqq! Msoxaz squark!" said the excited one.

"Ummmuh . . . rtyu . . . smoooog," replied the cautious one.

A tingly feeling raced up Matt's spine, and he slowly backed away from the door. What kind of people were in that room? And what were they doing in there?

Suddenly he heard another sound.

It was the whimpering of a dog.

Chapter

7

Matt lunged for the door and pounded on it with both fists.

"Dotti! Dotti! Are you in there?" Gulping, he cried, "Who are you? What are you doing to my dog?"

The voices stopped. The whimpering stopped. The whole inn seemed unnaturally silent. Only the wind howled outside.

Matt tried to swallow the lump of fear that was gathering in his throat. He knew it was Dotti he had heard. He'd know her whimper anywhere.

"Dotti!" he yelled again. "Dotti, where are you?"

Still, silence hung in the air.

Suddenly the door opened a crack. Matt's eyes widened in alarm as Dotti scampered out the narrow opening and into the hall, her tail between her legs. She let out a yelp when she saw Matt.

"It's okay, girl! Are you all right?" He dropped to one knee to pet her, but she took off at a gallop.

Matt raced after her. She careened around furniture in the lobby in her madcap dash for the stairway. He bounded up the stairs behind her and reached the top in time to see her crash through the half-open door to his room.

Out of breath, he stumbled into the room and collapsed against the bed. Dotti was cowering in the corner, her nose buried between her paws and her eyes wide with fright.

"It's okay, girl. Nobody's going to hurt you," he said. "Here, Dotti. Here, girl," he coaxed.

Dotti didn't budge.

Wrapping his arms around his pet, he asked softly, "What did they do to you in there?" He rubbed the top of her head while tears filled his eyes and terrible fear filled his heart.

All of a sudden his eyes focused on a small bare spot on the side of her head, just below her ear. He leaned forward and examined it. The white fur between two black spots had been shaved off a tiny area, not more than a square inch in size.

Gasping, he turned her head to the other side. An identical square-inch patch of bare skin was there, too.

"Oh, no!" he cried. "They really did do something to you!"

Matt started to jump to his feet to get help when he sank to the floor again. Had they done anything else to Dotti? If he looked her over carefully, would he find more marks?

Slowly and carefully, he went over every square inch of her body. Finally, on her left rear paw, he found what he had been afraid he'd find, a small cut in the shape of a half-moon.

Matt stared toward the window where snow still battered the glass. Something awful *was* going on at Snowed Inn. *But what was it?* He needed to tell his parents.

Pulling the leash out of his pocket, he reached for his ski jacket and put it on along with his mittens and cap. "Come on, girl," he coaxed again. "I need to talk to Mom and Dad. Then we'll go outside, and you can play in the snow."

This time Dotti scooted out from the corner and came to him, waiting patiently for Matt to snap the leash onto her collar.

When Matt got downstairs he spotted his parents coming out of the restaurant. But to his dismay, they were walking along and talking to Mrs. Rogers.

Rats, he thought. He didn't dare say anything in front of Mrs. Rogers until he found out more about what was going on. For all he knew, she might not be the sweet little grandmother she appeared to be. She could be in on it, too. She could even be the one who hurt Dotti!

The idea made him angry. He needed to talk to *somebody*. Looking around the lobby, he spotted Julee and Ashlee. But they were in a corner near the fireplace, deep in conversation with Lisa and Maggie. A glance toward the game room located Bart, busy at a video game with his back to Matt. He certainly didn't want to talk to him!

Matt decided that what he probably needed anyway was time to think before he approached his parents. And Dotti definitely needed to go outside.

A blast of icy air hit Matt as he opened the door and stepped into the snowstorm. Although it was cold, it seemed almost refreshing after the long night and scary morning inside Snowed Inn. He caught a snowflake on his tongue and let Dotti off the leash, watching her bound through the giant snowbanks.

Scrambling over the snow blocking the front stairs, Matt cut through the empty parking lot and headed toward the road. Dotti was running and barking ahead, woofing for him to hurry up. The road hadn't been plowed, and walking was hard. Puffing and panting, Matt had to struggle to keep from losing sight of his dog.

Poor Dotti, he thought. *What did they do to her?*

Unexpectedly Matt rounded a turn and was out of sight of the inn. He gasped and skidded to a stop.

He was standing in warm sunshine! And the road ahead was clear! The last of the snow was melting and trickling off into the ditches on both sides of the road, making soft little gurgling sounds.

He whirled around and looked back in the direction he had just come from. The blizzard was raging as hard as ever inside a giant cloud that reached from the ground beneath his feet to high into the sky above his head.

He turned again and whistled low in disbelief as he scanned the sky in the other direction. It was clear and blue for as far as he could see.

He stood frozen to the spot, his heart beating wildly.

Chapter

"What's going on?" Matt cried in bewilderment.

The only answer he got was the sound of Dotti lapping at a puddle.

He blinked two or three times. Then he rubbed his eyes. Was he dreaming?

No! he thought emphatically. *I'm wide-awake.*

Suddenly he wanted to run. He wanted to go tearing down that country road until he was as far away from Snowed Inn as he could get. He wanted to find civilization and someone who would come back with him and see the blizzard and tell him he wasn't crazy.

But he knew he couldn't leave to get help. His parents and the twins were inside the storm. What if he couldn't find his way back and something awful happened to them?

Matt slowly approached the cloud of snow. He stopped a couple of feet in front of it and stared into the wall of swirling whiteness. Then very slowly he reached a finger toward it, poking it quickly and jumping back as he touched the icy coldness.

It was real, all right. An honest-to-goodness snowstorm in the middle of a sunny landscape.

"Come on, Dotti," he said, sighing in resignation. "We've got to go back in. Let's go get Mom and Dad and Julee and Ashlee. We can get our things, come back here, and head for home."

Dotti jumped up and trotted toward the snow cloud. She sniffed around the edges, growling softly, but when Matt lowered his head and plunged into the storm, Dotti followed. Matt paused for an instant. Half his body was still in the warm sunshine. The other half was in the icy blizzard. Shaking his head in amazement, he hurried on toward the inn.

The big double doors creaked when he opened them. He stepped inside and stamped snow off his shoes. Beside him, Dotti shook and shimmied from the end of her nose to the tip of her tail, showering him with water.

He looked around the big lobby and saw to his

surprise that his father was the only one there. He was standing with his back to Matt, staring into the fire. The inn seemed eerily quiet. Bart and Lisa and Maggie weren't even in the game room.

"Dad!" Matt shouted, hurrying to him. "We can go home. I know how to get out of the storm."

"You must be mistaken," said a solemn masculine voice, and when the man turned around, Matt saw that it wasn't his father after all. It was Mr. Rogers.

"I thought . . . I mean . . . From the back you looked . . ." Matt fumbled for words. He could have sworn it was his dad. Even now Mr. Rogers looked more like his father than the Mr. Rogers he'd seen before. Maybe it was because he had changed from his cardigan sweater to a ski sweater like the one Matt's father usually wore.

"Why, all you have to do is look out the window to see that it's still snowing, and the weather report—" Mr. Rogers went on.

"I don't care what the weather report says," Matt insisted.

Just then his mother and father came out of the dining room.

"Mom! Dad! Listen to this! Dotti and I just went for a walk down the road. I know it sounds crazy, but down there the sun is shining and the snow is melting. We saw it! Not only that, we were *in* the sunshine for a minute. Dotti even got a drink of melted snow from a puddle."

Mr. Rogers scowled. "Young people have such imaginations, don't they?"

Then he snapped his fingers. Instantly a man Matt hadn't seen before appeared from behind Matt's back. Mr. Rogers whispered something to him. Nodding curtly, the man immediately disappeared down the short hallway where Matt had heard the mysterious voices and found Dotti earlier that morning.

Matt strained to see down the hall as the man opened the doors at the end and went inside. For the fraction of a second the doors were open, Matt was sure he heard the same humming he had heard when he woke up that morning, only louder. Was the furnace in there instead of in the cellar?

Mr. Rogers was still talking to Matt's parents. "Poor child must have cabin fever from being cooped up," he said with a little laugh. "Or maybe he was asleep and had a dream that the storm was over."

"Sleeping in my coat, hat, and gloves? Get serious," Matt grumbled. "And look how wet Dotti's and my feet are. Did we dream that, too?"

"Matt, where are your manners?" scolded his mother. "You mustn't talk to Mr. Rogers that way. He's only trying to help."

48

Matt looked up reluctantly. He knew his mother would never let up until he apologized to Mr. Rogers. But Mr. Rogers's attention had been drawn away from Matt. The man had come back from his errand. He nodded to Mr. Rogers, and the desk clerk was suddenly all smiles.

"I know what let's do," he said cheerfully. "Let's find out what this fine lad saw—or thinks he saw. I'll bring the four-wheel drive around from where it's parked behind the inn, and we'll check out Matt's story. It's only fair, don't you think?"

Matt's parents hurried to get their snow gear on and returned to Matt, who was waiting by the front door.

"The girls didn't want to go out in the storm, so they're staying here and playing with Dotti," said his father. "I can't say that I'm all that anxious to go out in this weather myself."

"Just wait," said Matt. "You'll see."

A moment later a blue four-wheel-drive Ford Bronco inched through the snowdrifts and stopped outside the front door. Matt and his parents piled in.

"You sit in the front seat with me, Matt, and show me where to go," Mr. Rogers said pleasantly.

Matt had a spooky feeling as he climbed into the car. Something about Mr. Rogers bothered him. Had he known all along that the blizzard only covered

Snowed Inn? And if so, why had he changed his tune so fast about checking it out?

Matt directed Mr. Rogers through the blinding snow. His and Dotti's footprints had long been lost in the thickening white stuff. In fact, the landscape was changing so fast as the wind blew the drifts around that Matt only hoped he'd be able to find the spot where he and Dotti had stepped into sunlight.

"Over there! Turn that way!" Matt shouted when he saw a familiar landmark. "It's just around that bend."

Mr. Rogers barely navigated the turn into a road that was covered with a foot of snow. The Bronco slid and skidded, almost plowing into a snowbank.

Matt was surprised to see that Mr. Rogers was gritting his teeth and gripping the steering wheel nervously. Wouldn't someone who operated an inn in the middle of ski country be used to driving in the snow? Matt was dying to point out Mr. Rogers's lack of driving skills to his dad and ask what he thought, but Mr. Meyers was in the backseat, and Matt couldn't say anything to him without Mr. Rogers overhearing.

"Well, where is this sunshine you insisted you saw?" asked Mr. Rogers.

"Just a little farther," said Matt. "I know it's right up here."

The Bronco slid again, this time almost slamming into a tree. It came to a stop just inches from the trunk. Mr. Rogers put the car in reverse, spinning wheels as he desperately tried to back it up. But the car was stuck.

Matt, his father, and Mr. Rogers got out of the car, and after a lot of heaving and straining, the three of them were able to push the vehicle onto the road again.

"Son, I think it's time we turn back," said his father in a weary voice. "We're not going to find any sunshine out here. I'm afraid I have to agree with Mr. Rogers that you dreamed it."

"But I didn't! I saw sunshine and a clear road!" Matt protested.

He sat slumped against the door as the vehicle headed back toward Snowed Inn. No one was listening. No one had believed a word he'd said.

I didn't dream it! he thought as tears of frustration gathered in his eyes. *I saw it, and Dotti saw it. We're just going to have to find it again!*

Chapter

Matt hung around on the front porch of the inn until he was sure his parents had gone upstairs and Mr. Rogers had taken the Bronco around back. He didn't want any of their I-told-you-so looks.

His face was numb from the cold, and his fingers were becoming stiff as he stood there, trying to think up a plan. He had to take someone with him when he went back to find the sunshine. That was the problem. He knew his parents wouldn't go. They were convinced it was a wild-goose chase. The twins wouldn't even go in the car, so there was no chance he'd get them to trudge through the snow.

That left only Bart.

Matt groaned. Bart would probably spend the

whole time asking Matt a million more questions. But there was no one else.

Matt plastered a fake smile on his face and headed for the game room. It might be worth a try.

"So, whatcha been doing?" asked Matt, trying his best to sound casual.

"Playing these stupid games," said Bart. "Man, I'm getting sick of them. I wish they'd get some new ones."

Matt brightened. "Hey, I know something we could do. We could go out and play in the snow."

Bart screwed up his face in a scowl. "Are you crazy? It's freezing out there."

"You get used to it after you're out there a little while," said Matt. "And it's pretty cool the way the snow's coming down. Sometimes, when the wind's really strong, it's almost horizontal. Come on. I'll show you. And we could build a snowman while we're out there."

Bart gave him a puzzled look. "A snowman?"

"Yeah, you know, a big snowball for a body, a medium-size snowball for a chest, and a little snowball for a head," Matt said, and snorted. "Give me a break."

"Forget it," grumbled Bart. "Let's go to the dining room and order some hot chocolate instead."

"Would you come outside with me if I promised to

53

show you something unbelievable? It'll knock your socks off," Matt said, grinning.

"Why would I want something to knock my socks off?" asked Bart. "What is it, anyway?"

"So, I got your attention, huh? If you want to find out, you'll have to come with me," said Matt.

"Why don't we stay in where it's warm and talk? What's your school like, anyway?" Bart began.

Matt threw him a disgusted look. "I haven't been there in so long I've forgotten," he said, but his sarcasm didn't seem to faze Bart. Or stop his questions.

"So what kind of music do you listen to?" Bart went on. "I like Tommy Dorsey. He's the king of swing."

"Swing? What's that?" asked Matt.

"You know, stuff like 'In the Mood.' That's a groovy song," said Bart.

Matt looked at Bart. He was really a strange one. Nobody he knew said *groovy* except his grandparents.

"Come on, Bart," Matt urged. "Let's go out and build that snowman. It's boring in here."

The boys bundled up in their jackets, hats, scarves, and gloves and headed out into the storm.

Matt pulled his scarf up over his nose and shivered as snow stung his face. Leaning into the wind, he headed toward the road as fast as he could. Bart loped along beside him.

"Where're we going?" yelled Bart, the sound of his voice almost lost in the howl of the wind. "I thought we were going to build a snowman."

"I promised to show you something, remember?" Matt said.

Bart trudged along beside Matt in silence. He didn't even ask any more questions. Matt was glad. He didn't feel like answering any. He had to concentrate on finding the sunshine again.

It took all his energy to keep going forward. The exertion was making him sweat inside his heavy clothes, the way it did sometimes when he skied hard.

Bart didn't seem to be having any trouble keeping up. In fact, he almost seemed to glide through the snow. Still, he didn't look very happy.

"I want to turn back," he shouted above the gale. "It's stupid to be out here in this when we could be back at the warm inn playing video games."

"I thought you were sick of those video games," Matt shouted back.

"Well, I'm sick of this, too! Didn't you hear me? I said I want to go back!" Bart grabbed Matt's sleeve and pulled him to a stop knee-deep in a snowdrift.

"Get your hands off me!" Matt demanded. He

jerked loose from Bart. "I can go anywhere I want to. Where do you get off telling me I can't."

"I just don't think we should go any farther, that's all," said Bart.

"Go back by yourself, then," grumbled Matt. He really wanted Bart to stay with him so that he'd have someone to back up his story if he found the sunshine again, but he definitely wasn't going to let Bart talk him into turning around. He had to try one more time to find a way out of the blizzard.

Bart got a strange look on his face. "You'll be sorry," he said, but instead of turning around, he started heading forward in the same direction they had been walking.

Matt hurried to catch up. Bart was pretty weird, but that didn't matter now. What mattered was that he'd be able to back up Matt's story about the sunshine, *if* he could find it again.

They walked along in silence for a few minutes. Matt was beginning to feel discouraged. It hadn't seemed this far from the inn before.

Just then he noticed a glow up ahead. It was as if the sun were trying to break through a thick fog.

"Sunshine!" he shouted as he struggled toward it through the snowbanks. "It's getting lighter. I know it's the sunshine! Look! There it is!"

Suddenly he smacked against something hard—

hard enough to knock him backward. He lay in the snow, rubbing his aching nose and staring in disbelief. He could see the sunshine! It was just in front of him!

Cautiously he reached toward it. Something stopped his hand. Something invisible. Like a glass wall. Or a giant bubble. On the other side were blue skies and a clear road.

Where had it come from? It hadn't been there before. When he had come to this spot the other time, he had been able to walk right out into the sunshine. And so had Dotti. She had even gotten a drink from a puddle.

Matt gasped. There was no way he could get out this time. He was trapped inside the blizzard!

Behind him, Bart was laughing like crazy.

Chapter

Matt jumped to his feet.

"What's going on?" he cried, looking frantically from Bart to the invisible wall and back to Bart again.

Bart was bent double with laughter.

Matt turned back to the wall in a panic, pounding on it with his fists. He had to break through! He had to get out of there!

When the wall didn't break, he kicked it as hard as he could. He could hear himself grunting as he heaved all of his weight against it. But it didn't give.

"Bart! I'm warning you! If you know what's—" he cried, spinning around. But Bart was gone.

Matt stared at the spot where Bart had been standing only seconds ago. He was panting furiously as he tried to get a grip on himself. It wouldn't do any good to go berserk. He had to try to figure things out on his own.

Finally, as his breathing slowed down to normal, he took the glove off his right hand and pressed the bare hand against the invisible wall. It felt hard and warm, like sunshine coming through a thick windowpane.

But what was the wall? How had it gotten there?

He started walking along beside it, feeling it with his hand and trying to see if it had a beginning or an end or maybe just a small opening that he could squeeze through. After a quarter of a mile or so without finding anything, he turned around and followed his tracks back to where he had started. With a sinking feeling in the pit of his stomach, he walked roughly the same distance in the other direction before returning to his starting point in defeat. Maybe he could go over the top. He looked up, but the invisible prison reached as far as he could see into the sky.

It's as if someone turned a big cereal bowl upside down on top of the storm, and we're all trapped inside! he thought frantically.

Matt took off, hopping and bounding over the mounds of drifting snow. He had to find Bart. He'd get the truth out of him if he had to beat him to a pulp to do it.

59

Bart was waiting for him just a short distance away, leaning against a tree. His arms were folded across his chest, and he had an insolent grin on his face. As Matt got closer, he started laughing again.

"Boy, you should have seen the look on your face when you smacked into that wall," Bart said.

Matt lunged for him, but Bart was too quick.

"You'd better tell me what's going on around here if you know what's good for you!" Matt warned. He pulled off his gloves and doubled up his fists.

"You really want to know? Well, I'll tell you," Bart said sarcastically. "You're stuck in Snowed Inn forever."

"Wha—" Matt gasped. He whirled around. He could see the sunshine, shining brightly beyond the wall. He could see the road that could take him home. Away from this crazy inn and the weird people in it. Bart had to be wrong. It was some kind of sick joke.

"What are you talking about?" he demanded.

But when he turned back to Bart, he was gone again.

Matt was breathless when he reached Snowed Inn and staggered through the front door. The fire was burning merrily as if everything in the world were perfectly normal. His father was sitting to one side of it, deep in conversation with a couple of men. His mother was on the other side of the room, talking to two women.

He dashed to the game room. Bart wasn't there. Matt hurried back into the big lobby. To his amazement, his mother was sitting by herself now, reading a book.

"Mom! Where did Dad go? He was here a minute ago. I've got to talk to him!" he cried.

Just as he approached her, he noticed that his father was being led down a hall by the two men he had just been talking to. It was the same hall where he had heard the strange language and found Dotti scared out of her wits.

"Dad!" Matt cried, but his father didn't look around.

"Mom? Where are they taking Dad?" Matt asked in alarm.

Mrs. Meyers glanced toward the hall and smiled. "I don't know, dear. It was something about a revolutionary new computer they wanted to show him. He was very excited."

Matt's pulse quickened.

"Dad! Dad, don't go with them!" he yelled, racing down the hall.

Matt pounded furiously on the first door he came to. "DAD! DAD! DON'T LET THEM DO ANYTHING TO YOU!" he screamed.

There was no answer. He pressed an ear against the door, straining to hear anything. The strange language. His dad talking to the other men about the computer. *Anything!*

There was only silence.

Matt pounded on the door again and twisted the knob. It was locked. He rattled it hard and yanked, but the door wouldn't open.

He raced to the door across the hall and tried it, pounding and jerking on the doorknob.

"Dad! It's Matt! Answer me!"

But there was still no answer.

He raced to the next door and the next, frantically pounding and yelling for his dad.

Finally there was only one room remaining. It was the one with double doors at the end of the corridor. His knees turned to rubber as he approached it. His palms were sweaty. This had to be the room where they'd taken his father.

He took a deep breath, pressing an ear against one of the doors, and then jumped back in alarm. A loud humming sound came from the room, the same sound he had heard this morning when he had first awakened.

"I thought it was the heating system," he whispered to himself. "But it must have been their big, fancy computer."

Matt stared at the door. His mother had called it a *revolutionary* computer. That had to mean it could do something normal computers couldn't do. And whatever it was, it could be doing it to his dad—right now!

Chapter

"Mom! Mom!" Matt shouted, running back into the lobby. "We've got to find Dad!"

"What's wrong, dear?" asked Mrs. Meyers. She put down her book and looked at him with concern.

"Mom, there are weird things going on around this place!" The words were tumbling out. "There's an invisible wall around Snowed Inn, and we're trapped inside in a blizzard. The sun's shining out there, and the snow's all melted. And Dad's gone into a room where people speak a strange language and—"

"Matthew Meyers! Calm down and explain to me what all this gibberish is about," said his mother in a tone of exasperation.

Matt dropped onto the sofa beside her. He was panting with fear and excitement.

"It's true, Mom," he said as calmly as he could. "Snowed Inn is trapped inside some kind of gigantic bubble or invisible wall. And Bart says we're stuck here forever. But that's not all. Dad could be in danger. *Awful* danger. You've got to believe me! They did something to Dotti, and they could be doing the same thing to Dad!"

Matt felt tears welling up in his eyes, and he fought to hold them back. He couldn't cry! He had to make his mother believe him. She'd never believe a crybaby. And she seemed to be thinking over what he had just said.

Mrs. Meyers frowned. "Who, dear? And what did they do to Dotti? I thought she was upstairs in your room playing with the twins and Lisa and Maggie."

"She is. I mean, I guess she is, and I'm not sure who they are or what they did," Matt said, trying to keep his thoughts straight. "It was this morning, right after breakfast, when I said I was going to take her outside. I couldn't find her. I looked all over the inn, and then I went down the same hall where Dad just went."

He paused and looked fearfully toward the dark corridor. "I heard voices coming from one of the rooms. But they weren't regular voices. They were

64

talking in a funny-sounding language. And when I called Dotti, the door opened, and she came slinking out. She was scared out of her wits, and when I looked her over, she had two spots by her ears where her hair had been shaved and a moon-shaped cut on her paw. Whoever they were, they were doing some kind of experiments on her, Mom, and they could be doing them on Dad right now!"

"Matt, you've been playing too many of those outlandish video games," she said patiently. "I don't know what language the other guests were speaking, or what Dotti was doing in their room, but, dear, you really must stop letting your imagination run away with you." She shook her head slowly. "Invisible walls? Experiments? What will you think of next?"

"Mo-*om*!" Matt insisted. "Everything I've said is true! You've got to believe me! Dad's in danger!"

Her face brightened as she looked over Matt's shoulder. "Look, here comes your father now," she said. "He looks okay to me. He certainly doesn't look as if he's been in the evil clutches of someone doing experiments on him."

Matt whirled around. His father was walking toward them with a big smile on his face.

"Amazing," he said. "That machine is absolutely amazing."

"You see, dear. You father is fine," she said to Matt.

Then turning to her husband, she said, "Matt was worried that something bad had happened to you."

Mr. Meyers chuckled. "What could possibly happen to me in a wonderful place like this? You know, I'm really glad we stopped at Snowed Inn. It's so relaxing here that I don't care if we ever get home."

Matt swallowed hard. That wasn't his dad talking. He was always wound up and on the go. He was hard-driving and hardworking. Still, Matt had to admit to himself that his dad looked okay. In fact, he looked more relaxed than Matt had seen him in a long time.

"Hi, Matt. Whatcha doing?"

He looked around to see Julee standing beside him. He hadn't noticed her come up.

"I thought you and Ashlee were playing with Lisa and Maggie and Dotti in the room," Matt said.

"We were, but I sneaked out. All those girls do is ask questions. It's so boring! I don't even like them anymore," she said emphatically. Then, looking worried, she added, "Ashlee is still there, but I don't think she wants to stay."

Matt's ears pricked up. Lisa and Maggie were Bart's sisters. If he was in on the strange things going on around here, they probably were, too. "So what kind of questions do they ask?"

66

Julee screwed up her face. "That's the weird part. They were asking questions about Dotti. Stupid questions."

"Like what?"

"Like why she walks on four legs instead of two, and why she has a tail. Isn't that stupid? All dogs walk on four legs," Julee said, rolling her eyes in disgust. "And they all have tails!"

Matt tried to stay calm, but the skin on the back of his neck was starting to crawl. There had to be something wrong with any nine-year-old girl who asked why a dog walks on four legs and has a tail. He had to get Ashlee away from Lisa and Maggie.

"Julee, you stay here. I'm going to go—"

He stopped in mid-sentence. He had glanced toward his father while he was speaking to his sister and had done a double take. Mr. Meyers had sat down and now he appeared to be reading a book. *But he was holding it upside down!*

"Mom!" he said in a shaky voice. "Mom, look!"

His mother didn't answer. To his horror, she was walking away with the two women he'd seen her talking to a few minutes before. They were heading for the same hallway his father had disappeared into.

Matt shook his father's arm so hard the book fell to the floor. "Dad! We've got to stop Mom!" he demanded.

Mr. Meyers gave him a pleasant smile. "Come on, Matt, calm down. It's just her turn to look at their computer."

Matt's heart jumped with fright. "You can't let her go with those people! Mom doesn't know anything about computers! She doesn't understand them! She doesn't even *like* them!" he insisted.

"She does now," his father said, picking up his book and going back to his upside-down reading.

Chapter

"Dad! Dad, are you okay?" Matt asked breathlessly.

But it was pretty obvious to Matt that his father wasn't okay. Mr. Meyers was gazing at his upside-down book with a rapturous look on his face, as if he were having a wonderful dream with his eyes wide open.

And that wasn't all. A tiny square patch of something blue was stuck to the back of each of his hands, like small blue bandages.

Matt's heart banged in his chest like a loose shutter in a windstorm.

"They *did* do experiments!" he whispered under his breath.

"What's the matter, Matt?" asked Julee. "And

what's the matter with Dad? Is . . . is something *bad* wrong with him?"

Julee's voice startled Matt. He'd forgotten she was there.

She was looking up at him. Her eyes were wide with fright. One big tear poised for a second before it came spilling down her cheek.

"Nothing, Jul. I promise. Everything's cool," he said quickly, trying not to frighten her. "Hey, I'll bet I know what you'd like. Some hot chocolate. And I'll bet you could get some in the dining room."

She swiped away the tear as a smile broke over her face.

"Okay," she said happily, and skipped off in the direction of the dining room.

Matt turned back to his father. "Dad," he began in a deadly serious voice. "What happened to your hands?"

His father glanced down and looked surprised. He ran a finger over each of the bandages and shrugged. "Oh . . . I don't know. I'm always banging myself up."

"Let me see what's under the bandages," Matt said firmly.

Mr. Meyers looked bewildered. "What for?" he asked. "It's just a scrape. Or a cut. What's the big deal?"

"You've got it right, Dad," Matt assured him. "It is a big deal. Come on. Take the bandages off."

"Kids!" Mr. Meyers said with a grunt as he peeled the blue patch off the back of his left hand.

Matt sucked in his breath. Underneath the bandage was a freshly made half-moon cut!

"What happened in that room, Dad?" Matt demanded.

"Room?" asked Mr. Meyers. "Oh, you mean the room where the computer was? Oh . . ." He got a vague look on his face. "I just looked at their computer, I think."

"Tell me about the computer. Tell me everything you can remember, and do it fast! We've got to save Mom," Matt said in a trembling voice. He had to know what he was up against before he went after her.

"What are you talking about? We don't have to save your mother. She's fine. She's looking at that amazing computer," said his father.

Matt wanted to scream at his father, but he knew that would only make things worse.

"Why is it so amazing?" he asked instead. "Tell me everything you can remember about it."

Mr. Meyers gazed off into the distance and then shook his head. "Hmmmmm. Funny thing. I can't remember anything about it. Isn't that peculiar? But

71

ask your mother when she comes back," he added with a big grin. "She has a much better memory than I do."

Matt sat back and stared at his father. Things were even worse than he'd suspected. "Sure, Dad. I'll do that," he muttered.

He turned his attention to the hall. His mother had to be in the room with the double doors. The room where he'd heard the computer humming. The *revolutionary* computer. But how could he get inside to save her? He couldn't count on his dad's help. Someway they had messed with his mind. Matt had never felt so alone in his life.

He tried to swallow the wad of fear that was filling his throat. Maybe he should wait. Or try to get one of the other guests to help.

Matt sighed. Deep down he knew he couldn't do either. He didn't know who he could trust—if anybody! It was all up to him. He had to rescue his mother by himself, and he had to do it *now*.

Matt marched across the lobby, his head held high and his fists clenched as he tried to psych himself up. Passing the registration desk, he heard papers shuffling. He looked up to see Mr. Rogers smiling at him.

"You're a very smart young man, aren't you?" asked the clerk. "I'll bet you know all sorts of

interesting things. Can you spell the word
interesting?"

Matt stared at him. This was crazy!

"I don't have time," he mumbled, and tried to
hurry by.

Mr. Rogers stepped in front of him, looking at
him with steely determination. Matt tried to go
around him, but the desk clerk held out a hand and
stopped him.

"I *said*—" Mr. Rogers paused, letting the word
sink in, "can you spell *interesting*?"

"I-N-T-E-R-E-S-T-I-N-G," Matt spit the letters out.

"I knew you could," said Mr. Rogers, smiling
benevolently. Then he stepped behind his desk
again, letting Matt pass.

The instant he moved aside, Matt's mouth
dropped open, and he heard himself utter a
sorrowful moan. He was too late!

His mother was coming from the hallway and
walking slowly toward the sofa where his father was
sitting. She had a dreamy smile on her face and a
blue bandage on each of her hands.

Chapter

Matt watched in horror as his mother sat down beside his father. They grinned at each other like a pair of lovesick teenagers.

Seeing Matt, his mother called out, "Isn't this a romantic old inn? I just love it here! In fact, I wish it would snow for days and days so that we could stay and enjoy it longer."

"But what about me and the twins? We have to get back to school," he reminded her, even though he was afraid that he knew what she would say even before she said it.

"Don't worry about school," she said, smiling her dreamy smile. "You children can afford to miss a few more days. You're very good students."

Panic was rising in Matt. If only he could get through

to his parents and make them come to their senses. He had to convince them that they needed to escape from Snowed Inn as fast as they could. He didn't dare wonder what would happen to all of them if they didn't. But his parents were obviously in some kind of trance.

"What about your big project at work, Dad?" he asked hopefully. "I know how important it is and how much they really need you."

Mr. Meyers looked puzzled for an instant. "Project?" he said questioningly. "Oh, yes. There is a project, isn't there? Well, I think they can do without me. It's really not all that important."

With that, Mrs. Meyers gave her husband a reassuring nod and opened her book again. Sighing with contentment, they both began reading *upside down*.

Matt stared into the fire, his mind churning. He had to get into the room with the double doors. It had to hold the key to everything that was going on at Snowed Inn. And he had to do it right away. But the big question was, did he have the courage?

He made a quick survey of the almost empty lobby. A few people were lounging around on the comfortable furniture, some napping. Mr. Rogers had disappeared again. And then there were his parents, reading their upside-down books. They wouldn't notice if he slipped away. He had to do it. Now.

Matt hurried into the dark hallway. His heart was pounding. He had no idea how he was going to get into that room. He had never broken into a place before, and he certainly didn't know how to pick a lock.

Halfway down the hall he stopped and blinked hard at one of the double doors. Was it slightly ajar? Or was he seeing things?

He could hear the computer humming now, and the sound was definitely coming from inside the dark room. He dropped to a crouch and crept closer. The hum was getting louder. Suddenly he heard voices.

"Luxzk mbra pqac! Flofl zurkat krego!"

"Skyyyyy . . . zumm . . . boogur . . ."

Matt froze in his tracks. It was the same language he had heard when Dotti had come running out of that room. And the voices still sounded more mechanical than human.

"Zumit! Zumit! Zumit!" cried the young one.

"Draaaaabbbbb . . ." replied the older one.

Matt swallowed hard and moved toward the door. It was now or never. He was going to get some answers.

As he got closer to the opening, he became aware of soft lights inside, going on and off like strobes. It made him think of the game room. Did they repair video games in there? He cautiously pushed the door open farther, slid inside, and pressed himself against the wall.

The room was large and filled with electronic equipment and video screens. In front of the videos, there were slanted panels with all kinds of slide switches, dials, and levers.

"Kkwje jvvvvvvk!"

Matt shrank back in horror as a huge hologram of a Plyomith warrior went streaking past him, heading across the room. Matt moved quickly and hid himself deep in the shadows. He held his breath and watched a second warrior hologram turning a dial and pushing a lever on a panel in the wall. A large section of the panel opened up, revealing a window.

Matt gasped. Inside the window was a telescope, pointing toward the heavens. What he saw shocked him. There were clusters of stars, planets with rings around them, and swirling galaxies. He was looking into the dark recesses of outer space instead of at the grounds surrounding Snowed Inn!

Matt let his breath out as everything started to become clear. He had read about spaceships that landed on Earth and took humans aboard for experiments. He had always thought it was just science fiction or stories people made up to get their names in the newspaper. But this was real! He and his family weren't in a ski lodge. They were aboard an alien spacecraft that had landed in the ski country of rural Vermont! And this was the control room!

This had to be where the Plyomiths controlled the weather and kept the blizzard raging outside. And where they raised and lowered the invisible bubble to keep Matt and his family trapped inside. But why? What kind of terrible experiments were they performing? What did they want to find out?

"Uuuuuziw . . . frpsuuuug," said the second warrior, startling Matt, who was so deep in thought he had almost forgotten that the two holograms were there.

He didn't think either of them had seen him as he cringed in the darkness. Slowly his eyes were adjusting to the eerie lights in the room. He stared at the Plyomiths, frozen in terror. They seemed so real! His mind kept coming back to the same questions. What kind of experiments had they been conducting on his parents and Dotti? Did they plan to do experiments on him, too? And the twins?

"Oxneirt zapf!" the excited one said, and headed for the door leading back into the main part of the inn.

The other one nodded slowly and followed. "Fooooppppplle . . ." he said.

Just as the first Plyomith reached the door, it suddenly began to change, shrinking rapidly like a balloon losing air. The second one did the same thing.

Before Matt's astounded eyes, the figures blurred, and when their images cleared again they had turned into Mr. Rogers and Bart!

Chapter

The door closed behind Bart and Mr. Rogers, leaving Matt alone in the control room of the spacecraft. His knees were weak as he slowly crept out of his hiding place. He had to fight off an overwhelming urge to run away. To escape to someplace safe. But he knew there was no place that was safe as long as he was trapped in Snowed Inn.

He looked around the dim room. Lights blinked and pulsed, and video monitors glowed with strange images on the giant computer in the center of the room. He felt more frightened than ever.

Why had the Plyomiths landed on Earth? What did they want from Matt and his family? Had Bart been telling the truth when he said they were stuck in Snowed Inn *forever*?

Suddenly Matt had an idea. The mechanism that raised and lowered the invisible wall had to be somewhere in the computer. All he had to do was find it, raise the wall, and then convince his family to run for safety.

He whistled low. That wasn't going to be easy. Especially since his parents were in la-la land, and he suspected the other people at the inn—the guests, the football players, the waitress—were all members of the spacecraft's crew and could change their appearances the same way Bart and Mr. Rogers could. That would explain why there were never any other cars in the parking lot.

Instantly Matt realized that he had been standing in the same spot for several minutes. What if the Plyomiths came back and caught him there? He had to get busy.

He had no idea where to start. He glanced past the computer. The room was large, and there were other, smaller rooms off to the left of the main one.

Stepping up to the nearest electronic panel on the computer, he looked in wonder at the maze of dials, levers, and switches. Although there were symbols under most of them, he couldn't make them out.

They must be written in Plyomith, Matt thought.

Tentatively he turned the dial and pushed the lever he had seen the Plyomith turn and push when he first came into the room. Without a sound, the large wall panels started closing over the window to outer space. He turned the dial and moved the lever in the opposite direction and the window opened again.

A whirring noise coming from the next panel caught his attention, and he moved over to it. The sound was being made by several tiny gyroscopes in a long glass tube mounted in the panel. The gyroscopes seemed to be suspended in air and were spinning crazily and moving back and forth, constantly changing places.

The next panel had a monitor that was twice the size of the others. Bursts of colored lights flashed and streaked across the screen. Speakers were mounted on both sides of the monitor and strips of blinking lights and a red button were positioned under it. Matt reached out and pushed the button.

"Gwwpprrt! Glimft, glimft, zool, zool!" came a loud voice from the speakers. The blinking lights flashed wildly and the lights on the monitor flared brightly, lighting up the room. A solid white light appeared in its center.

"What the—" Startled, Matt jumped back.

Then he punched the button again. The lights on the screen dimmed, and the speakers grew silent.

He looked fearfully at the doors that led to the main part of the inn, expecting Mr. Rogers and Bart to come barging in.

To his relief, the doors remained closed.

Whew! I haven't seen a computer like that, either in real life or in science-fiction movies! he thought, looking at the lights. *This must be the monitor for the alien ship's power source!*

He decided not to push any more buttons or move any more levers, since he didn't know what would happen. Instead he went to check out the other rooms.

The first one looked like a bedroom with several beds, only the beds were silver cylinders with glass doors over the areas where the sleepers' heads would be. He had seen things like them in science-fiction movies. In the movies they were used for the aliens to sleep in while their ship was traveling to some far-off planet. While they were in the cylinders, their body temperatures would be lowered to near zero so that their body processes would slow down and they wouldn't get any older. He had studied about it in science class. It was called cryogenics.

Matt shivered at the thought that the Plyomiths must have come from a long way off to find him and his family. *Why?*

The next two rooms reminded Matt of hospital

operating rooms. In the center of each was a rectangular metal table with floodlights hanging above it. Surrounding the tables were stands with equipment boxes and more monitors mounted on them. Cables and wires were strung everywhere.

Matt suddenly had a sick feeling in the pit of his stomach.

Was this where my parents and Dotti were taken?

He looked at the equipment in amazement. He couldn't even begin to imagine what the Plyomiths had done to his parents and his dog.

Matt backed out of the room. He couldn't wait any longer to find a way to get his family out of Snowed Inn. There was no telling what the Plyomiths would do to them next.

Suddenly he heard a door opening. He leaped into the shadows and held his breath as he watched.

Julee and Ashlee were coming through the door with Lisa and Maggie. As the door closed, Lisa and Maggie began to grow and change. They got larger and larger, and their faces started to swell. Their eyes darkened, and their mouths turned down in evil sneers.

Matt watched in horror as his little sisters walked across the room, holding the hands of two giant Plyomiths!

Chapter

15

Julee and Ashlee were looking up at the two warriors, holding their hands and chattering happily, right before Matt's astonished eyes.

"And I just don't understand why they don't have television sets in the rooms here," Julee was saying.

He blinked and looked again. Why couldn't the twins realize that Lisa and Maggie had changed? Why couldn't they *see* the hideous Plyomiths who had led them into the room?

"I agree," said Ashlee. "You'd think there'd at least be one in the lobby."

He had to hold himself back to keep from jumping out from his hiding place. He doubled up his fists. He wanted to smash the monsters in the mouth and grab his sisters away from them. He sighed and sank deeper into the shadows. It was a stupid idea. He would be no match for the giant Plyomiths. Capturing him would be easy, and then they'd do the same things to him that they'd done to his mother and father. The same things they were getting ready to do to his sisters. If he got caught, there would be no hope at all—for any of them.

Matt watched helplessly as each Plyomith took one of his sisters into an operating-type room and helped her up onto a table. The girls giggled happily as they lay down and stretched out. They acted as if it were some kind of game.

"My favorite ice cream is chocolate crunch," Matt heard Ashlee telling the Plyomith who was standing over her.

"Glom du beaterrock," said the alien.

"Oh, I don't like that kind at all," responded Ashlee. "It's icky."

Matt couldn't believe his ears. His sister actually could understand the Plyomith language!

Matt watched in horrified fascination as Ashlee's warrior touched a switch that filled the room with an eerie green light. Next the Plyomith took a silver jar off a high shelf and opened it, smearing a clear gel over his hands, which he then spread on the backs of her hands.

He's going to cut half-moons into her hands! Matt thought frantically. *I've got to stop him!*

But instead, the Plyomith attached suction cups trailing tiny black wires to each hand.

When Matt threw a glance at Julee, the same thing was happening to her.

Matt's heart was beating madly. What were the experiments for?

When he looked again, the alien monsters were turning the girls' heads to one side and carefully running what looked like small electric razors against their heads just behind their ears, only the razors didn't make any sound. They did the same to the other sides of their heads and then attached electrodes to the shaved places.

Matt sank back on his heels and covered his eyes with his hands. His heart was bursting inside his chest. He felt so totally, bewilderingly helpless!

He looked around quickly when he heard movement in the room. Julee and Ashlee were up again and standing on the floor. They had the same dreamy smiles on their faces that his parents had had when they came from the room. It was as if they had *enjoyed* what had happened! And they each had blue bandages on the backs of their hands.

The Plyomiths led the girls to the door into the inn. As they approached the doors, the aliens began to shrink and blur and then develop human forms, just as Bart and Mr. Rogers had done before.

Matt knew exactly what was going to happen. He shook his head in wonder as the blurred figures turned back into Lisa and Maggie.

After they were gone, Matt stayed in his hiding place, too terrified to move.

"I'm next!" he whispered. "Bart and Mr. Rogers, and maybe even Lisa and Maggie, are probably looking for me at this very instant! And if they find me . . ." He looked back at the rooms where Ashlee and Julee had been just moments ago and shuddered. His eyes found the silver jar filled with gel and the switch that had produced the eerie green light.

What am I going to do? a voice screamed inside his brain. *How can I get all of us out of this terrible nightmare? What can I do against powerful aliens from outer space?*

Another question continued to hammer away in his mind. What did the Plyomiths want from his family? They wouldn't have come all this way and captured them just to poke around and attach a few wires. They had to have a purpose. A goal. *But what?*

All Matt knew was that whatever their reasons were, he had to stop them.

He stood up and set his jaw firmly. There had to be *something* he could do before they found him.

He had to at least try! He started frantically running his hands over the back of the equipment bay, searching desperately for a way to get it open.

Chapter

When Matt entered the game room half an hour later, Bart was playing Battling the M42 Plyomith Warrior. Matt hesitated at the door. He knew he was taking a terrible chance, but he didn't have any choice. He took a deep breath and went in.

He watched as Bart expertly pointed at a weapon, which immediately appeared in his hand. He quickly pointed and fired before the hologram warrior could even get a weapon. The hologram dissolved. Matt couldn't help wondering if the hologram in the game was really a member of the spacecraft's crew.

"Where have you been?" Bart asked, without looking around.

Matt's scalp prickled with fear. "Around," he said.

"Want to play?" asked Bart.

"Maybe," said Matt.

"Not afraid of losing again, are you?" asked Bart, turning and grinning at Matt.

Matt studied Bart closely. Somehow he didn't look the same. Matt was sure of that, but he couldn't quite figure out why.

He swallowed a lump in his throat and stepped forward to take Bart's place in front of the machine. Sucking in a deep breath, he took a moment to settle himself down. Then he jabbed at the start button, pointed at a weapon that looked like a TV remote, and fired it at the warrior as soon as it appeared in his hand.

The blast caught the hologram as it was wheeling to fire at Matt. The hologram gave out a terrific shriek that made Matt jump back in alarm, and then it disappeared in a flash of light.

"How come he didn't make that sound when you shot him?" Matt asked Bart.

Bart pulled his eyes away from where the hologram had been. He looked at Matt a minute before answering.

"It's a Plyomith game. It only does that if a non-Plyomith shoots him. He doesn't like being shot by a non-Plyomith. I know another game you'd like, but it's not here," said Bart.

90

A chill went up Matt's spine. Bart was admitting he was a Plyomith. He was also starting to make his move on Matt.

"Where's the other game?" he asked cautiously.

"In another room at the back of the inn," Bart said casually. "It's right down the hall. Wanna go see it?"

Matt worked up the silliest smile he could manage. "I think I've already seen it."

Bart looked surprised. "You what? Who showed it to you?"

Matt glanced over his shoulder. Mr. Rogers was nowhere in sight. He decided to take a chance.

"Mr. Rogers," Matt said.

Bart narrowed his eyes and looked hard at Matt. "He did?"

Matt tried to conjure up an even bigger smiley face, like the ones he'd seen on his parents after they'd come from the experiments. "Yes, he did, and it was cool."

Bart glanced down at Matt's hands and frowned at the blue bandage on the back of each one. He shrugged. "Darn! He said I could do you."

"I really feel terrific since I played the game in the other room," said Matt. "Can I go back there again?"

"Since you've been there once, you'll have to wait your turn to go again," answered Bart, frowning again. "Your time will come, though. Trust me. And I'll make sure I get to do you next time. It'll be even more fun. You'll see."

Matt tried to grin even more widely, but his mouth wouldn't stretch any farther. Bart seemed to be fooled, but Matt couldn't be sure. He had to lay his act on even thicker.

"I feel like reading," he said in his best la-la voice.

He picked up a business magazine from a table, went over to one of the big chairs, and plunked down in it. Holding the magazine upside down, he pretended to read. He only hoped Bart bought his act and believed that Matt had been taken into the spacecraft's control room and experimented on. It was the only chance he had to buy time and finish working out his escape plan.

He held the magazine up in front of his face and surveyed the room over the top of it. Ashlee, Julee, Lisa, and Maggie were together on a couch near the fireplace, talking. His parents were sitting on another couch, deep in conversation with Mrs. Rogers. Just then Mr. Rogers came in and sat down beside them.

If I didn't know what horrible things those monsters are doing to my family, I'd think they were just a bunch of friends, sitting around and talking, he thought. *They all look so happy. And they look—*

Matt almost dropped his magazine. His hands trembled as a horrible realization came over him. *They looked alike!*

Mr. Rogers appeared identical to Matt's father. They could have been twins! Mr. Rogers even had on jeans and a ski sweater just like Matt's dad, instead of slacks and a cardigan sweater. And Mr. Rogers looked more ruddy and more muscular than he had before. Like a man who enjoyed outdoor sports.

Matt turned his eyes toward Mrs. Rogers. Not only did her hair seem to have changed from gray to blond, the same shade as Matt's mother's hair, but she was wearing a black and gold jogging suit identical to his mother's. That wasn't all about the two that was the same. Matt blinked. It was almost as if his mother were sitting beside herself!

But Mr. and Mrs. Rogers hadn't looked that way when Matt's family first arrived at Snowed Inn!

Matt jerked around and stared at the girls. Lisa and Maggie were the exact images of Julee and Ashlee. They could have been quadruplets.

Matt forced himself to look at Bart, who was standing outside the game room. He was leaning against the door frame watching Matt and his family. Suddenly Matt understood what had seemed strange about him before.

Looking at Bart now was like looking into a mirror!

Chapter

17

"Oh, Dotti, what am I going to do? If only you could talk and help me figure out how we're going to get out of this mess," Matt said, hugging his pet close.

Matt hadn't been able to bear seeing the results of the Plyomiths' transformation from huge, ugly aliens to creatures who looked like duplicates of his family. He had come back to his room where he could lie on the bed and think. But his brain was paralyzed with fear. He turned over on his stomach and pounded the bed in frustration.

What am I going to do? I couldn't find the power source for the computer! I can't fight the Plyomiths! They're a lot bigger than me, and they have powerful weapons! I have nothing! I'm just a kid!

And time had to be running out. Bart had told

him that he would have to wait his turn to go back into the room at the end of the hall. Naturally that meant they would be taking his family back in there first to do more experiments.

They had already made his father forget about his job and the big project he was working on. And his mother would never have allowed him and his sisters to miss a day of school unless they were sick and about to die. But now, she didn't care. She wanted to stay snowed in at Snowed Inn! It was as if his parents had completely forgotten about their home and the life they'd had before they came to Snowed Inn.

What do the Plyomiths have in store for us next? The question sent shivers up his spine. He didn't want to even try to imagine the things they might do. He just wanted to get his family out of there.

Dotti whimpered and snuggled close to him. Matt looked down at her, and tears came to his eyes. The monster aliens were even doing things to good old Dotti. Maybe *he* hadn't always been on his best behavior, Matt had to admit, but his dog had never hurt a thing in her life. She wouldn't even chase cats!

His jaw was set with determination when he went downstairs with Dotti a short while later. As soon as he entered the main room he sensed something else was wrong. When he had left to go upstairs, his family had all been talking to their mirror images.

Now the room was silent.

Quickly he glanced around. Ashlee and Julee were sitting up straight in overstuffed chairs, while the other two girls sat on the floor playing a game. His sisters' jaws were slack, and their eyes looked glazed, as if they were sleeping with their eyes open. His mother was on the couch, sitting beside the woman he thought was Mrs. Rogers, staring absently into the fire.

Matt gulped hard. His family all appeared to be in a world of their own.

"Hey, everybody! What's going on?" he called, but no one answered.

Suddenly he took a closer look at the two women. The one on the right *was* his mother, wasn't she? He shook his head. They looked so much alike, he wasn't sure anymore. Maybe the woman with the dazed look was Mrs. Rogers and the other one was his mother. Then why didn't she seem to recognize him? What was happening?

"Mom? Mom!" he shouted. "It's me! Matt!"

He spun toward his sisters and the other two girls, staring hard. Which ones were Julee and Ashlee? He couldn't tell that either.

His mind was whirling. Even if he found a way to get his family out of there, he wouldn't know which ones to take with him!

Matt heard the sound of a door closing and wheeled around to see two men who looked just like his father come out of the hall. One of them plodded along like a zombie, and the other man held on to his arm and guided him. Matt watched as they came into the main room and one of them directed the other to sit down.

"DAD!" he screamed. "Dad, listen to me! You've got to snap out of this! It's a matter of *life and death*!"

But if his father heard, he didn't let on.

Slowly Matt's mind seemed to clear as he began to understand what was happening. The aliens were duplicating his parents' bodies, all right, but they were also emptying their minds. *The Plyomiths were stealing his family's identities!*

Why? What did they want? And worst of all, what would the aliens do with all of them when they had everything they wanted? Throw them away like empty peanut shells?

Matt felt someone looking at him. He knew who it was before he turned around.

Bart was staring straight at him, smiling triumphantly.

Chapter

"You've figured it out, haven't you?" asked Bart.

"Figured out what?" Matt faked a dreamy smile so Bart would think he was under the Plyomiths' power.

"Don't try to kid me!" Bart said, and sneered. "Let me see your hands."

Matt backed away, but he wasn't fast enough. Bart reached out and tore the blue bandage off the back of Matt's right hand.

"Aha! See! Just as I suspected. You lied. You *haven't* been to the back room yet! Brwwgke hasn't done you, after all."

"Who's Brw-w-ke?" Matt stumbled over the strange-sounding word. "Or whoever you said."

"Brwwgke," replied Bart, rolling his eyes to show his disgust. "You're so inferior you can't even pronounce a simple Plyomith word like *Brwwgke*."

"Who cares!" Matt shouted angrily. "I was too in the back room. The little cuts on my hands have just healed, that's all."

"You never had cuts on your hands," said Bart. "They can't heal. They're little flaps of skin where the sensors were inserted to drain your memories. And you also don't have shaved patches for attaching electrodes to the sides of your head. The Blemowac says you haven't been done yet."

"The Blemowac? What's that?" asked Matt.

"You're really stupid, aren't you?" Bart said with a snort. "In your Earthling language the Blemowac is a computer. But it's not like any computer you poor, inferior creatures ever imagined. Watch this!"

Suddenly Bart wasn't Bart anymore, or even a clone of Matt. His form got blurry as he expanded, growing bigger and bigger until he had turned into a hideous Plyomith warrior.

"Let's see *you* do that," challenged the monster. His voice had changed, too. Now it was the high-pitched sound of the younger Plyomith that Matt had heard in the control room.

"You can't, can you?" The alien let out a sinister laugh. "Besides guiding our spaceship throughout the universe, the Blemowac allows us to create hologram images around our bodies so we can take on whatever appearances we want. But those aren't the only holograms we make. Our spaceship landed here during a snowstorm, so we turned it into a hologram of a ski lodge, which we appropriately named Snowed Inn." He paused, chuckling at the joke. "Then we made sure the storm continued once you and your family were inside, so we made a hologram of that, too."

"So that was it!" Matt shouted. Now more things were making sense. "And when I found a way out of the storm, you had to do something to keep me in. That's when you put down the invisible wall! But why do you want to look like us? And why are you keeping us here?"

"We could have made ourselves look like you and your family the instant you came here if we had wanted to. But we needed your cooperation until we had time to test you and find out all there is to know about you—which isn't much," the alien monster said with a snicker. "We are so superior to you Earthlings."

"But you still haven't answered my question. Why do you want to do this to us? We never did anything to you or your planet," insisted Matt.

The Plyomith warrior threw back his head and

laughed. His voice echoed off the ceiling. "Of course you haven't done anything to planet M42, as you Earthlings call it. Your race is too weak, puny one. Planet M42 is twenty million light-years away. You could never have traveled so far. Not in your biggest and best spaceship."

He paused and looked at Dotti. "At first we thought *that* thing might be the superior race on this planet," he said, sniffing in disdain. "It would have been good for us if it were. Our sensors tell us it is incapable of fighting back. It would have made things so much easier for us."

"Leave Dotti alone," pleaded Matt. "And please just let us go."

"We plan to do just that as soon as we're finished with you," said the alien, a red light flaring in his evil eyes. "Which won't make you very happy either, I'm afraid. When the time comes, we're going to take the useless shells of your bodies up into space and jettison them into a black hole."

Matt gulped. His heart felt like a pile driver inside his chest. "What have you done to my mother and father? What are you doing to my sisters?"

"Okay, let me spell it out for you," said the Plyomith. "All the resources on our planet have been used up. It's worn out. It can no longer support our race, and many are dead. We need another home.

"We learned much about Earth from the occasional radio and television transmissions that reached us in deep space. That is how we knew about the famous Simpson family and Mr. Rogers. We assumed their identities because you Earthlings admire them so much. But the few transmissions we got were not enough. There was not enough information in them for us to learn enough to survive on Earth. We had to learn more. We had to fill in the blanks—as you Earthlings say."

He paused as if to let the horrible reality sink in to Matt's mind.

"You mean . . . like finding out what a mall is? And a beach?" Matt asked in a faltering voice.

The Plyomith nodded. "We had another problem, also. There are many of you and few of us. If all our people tried to come at once and overpower you, there would be a war. Although we have superior brains and superior weapons, some of us could get killed, no matter how *puny* you are.

"So instead, we're coming a few at a time. We're changing ourselves to look, act, and talk like you, one by one. And then we'll take over your lives. We'll move into your houses. We'll go to your jobs and your schools. And the beauty of it is, no one will ever suspect that we aren't you!"

The alien's eyes gleamed. "Your family is the first

to be done because you wandered into our trap. When we are in place in our new identities, we'll set up more traps. Then we'll signal for the rest of the surviving Plyomiths to begin coming. They are only waiting for our signal."

Matt stared at the alien. This was real. It wasn't just a bad dream. He wasn't going to wake up and find himself in his own bed at home. This hideous Plyomith would!

A cold sweat of fear came over Matt. "My mom and dad? My sisters? They're going to be this way forever?"

The monster gave him a defiant look. "Of course. The only possible way they could be changed back is if the Blemowac were to be turned off. Then all the information gathered from their brains and stored in the Blemowac would reverse and flow back out and into their bodies again. But don't get any ideas. There's no way that can happen. The Blemowac has an eternal power source built inside, and there are no switches to turn it on and off. Do you want to watch your sisters being done for the final time while you're waiting your turn? You may find it as amusing as I do."

Matt felt as if he were going to throw up. His hands were clammy and his head throbbed. He had to destroy the Blemowac. But he couldn't. There was absolutely nothing he could do!

But his sisters! He suddenly knew he had to see them one more time before . . . before the aliens did him. He had to say good-bye and tell them he was sorry he couldn't save them—even if they couldn't hear him. It was the only thing left to do.

With a deep sigh, he followed the Plyomith down the hall with Dotti slinking along at his heels.

Chapter

19

The alien pushed open the door to the control room. With a heavy heart, Matt followed him inside. Dotti went in, too. Five or six Plyomiths were in the main room, turning dials and pushing levers. Matt glanced at them, wondering briefly which ones were the football players, the waitress, and the other guests. They all looked alike.

The panel was open over the window, and Matt could see deep space. A brilliant light that Matt hadn't seen before was in the center of the blackness, pulsing brightly in the center of the window.

"That is our planet M42," the Plyomith who had been Bart said proudly. "Our people are watching—waiting for us to complete our mission and send for them."

Matt shuddered at the thought of thousands—maybe millions— of Plyomiths watching his and his family's destruction. He looked away abruptly and began scanning the control room. He couldn't stop looking for a way out as long as he had one more breath left.

The largest equipment-panel screen, which had been filled with streaks of lights when Matt had sneaked in earlier, was now filled with a myriad of glowing dots. They were bouncing and moving from side to side, up and down, and round and round in crazy patterns. Dots disappeared, and others took their place.

One Plyomith had apparently seen the puzzled look on Matt's face.

"The Blemowac is sending our friends on M42 a progress report. They're very happy with what we've accomplished in so short a time, and they are very anxious to join us."

Matt glanced fearfully at the alien. Time was running out. In a few minutes he would be a zombie just like the rest of his family, and the Plyomiths would begin taking over the world. His only hope was to disable their computer, but there was no way he could do that with no external way to turn it off.

Suddenly his attention was drawn to one of the hospital rooms. His sisters! He had almost forgotten them in his worry about the computer. He rushed into the room, his heart beating wildly.

Two small forms were lying on metal tables. One was Ashlee and the other Julee. There was no doubt this time that he was seeing his sisters.

Their faces were pale, their eyes closed. Wires hanging from boxes in the ceiling were connected to the girls' hands and heads. Instantly the monitors lit up. Some had ziggy lines, others had columns of lights that rose and fell on the screens. The monitor in the middle had streaks of color radiating from a white center that grew large enough to fill the screen and then quickly shrank away to almost nothing.

As Matt stared in horror at the two lifeless forms, someone chuckled behind him.

"The Blemowac is doing a great job," said the alien. "It won't be long until your sisters will be done. Then you can hop up onto a table and take your turn. I will do you myself!"

"I hate you!" Matt spit out in frustration. "I hate you, Bart Simpson, or Plyomith warrior, or whoever you are! You've got no right coming to our planet and doing this to us!"

"Oh, but we have," the alien assured him. "We're bigger and stronger than you. You have a saying. Something about survival of the fittest. Do you remember that?"

Matt ignored the Plyomith's question. "You probably think you're stronger and smarter than everyone in the entire universe," Matt said. "I'll bet somewhere out there are people who are a lot stronger and know a lot more than you do. Someday you're going to run into them. And you'll be sorry."

Matt could feel anger and frustration welling inside him. He hated these monsters for capturing his family and sucking out their spirit and personalities, leaving them like empty eggshells.

Numbly he watched the Plyomiths disconnect the wires from Ashlee and Julee. The ziggy lines and the growing columns on the monitor screens stopped moving. The streaks of lights on the main monitor settled down, too. Then the aliens lifted the girls off the tables and stood them on the floor.

Matt stared helplessly into their blank faces and vacant eyes. They had the same expressions he'd seen on his parents' faces. He wanted to cry. His sisters looked totally and completely mindless.

"All done," the monster said cheerfully. "The Blemowac can control them now through the sensors we've planted in them. We won't need the wires anymore. Any other information we need transferred to us can be done automatically. Now it's your turn."

"*No way*! shouted Matt, knocking the alien's hand away. "I'm not going to let you touch me!"

"Bor-*ring*," said the Plyomith as he pulled a

weapon from his belt. It looked like the one Matt had used in the Battling the Plyomith Warrior game. "Stop me if you can, puny one."

Matt looked frantically first at him and then at his weapon. Should he make one last try and grab for it? Would the monster shoot him if he did? The loss of one Earthling wouldn't make any difference. They could always get another one.

Just then he heard a growl behind him.

Suddenly Dotti came bounding across the room, a blur of black and white and gleaming fangs. She was still ten feet away when she leaped into the air and hit the alien, grabbing his wrist in her teeth.

"*Drraomaeap!*" shrieked the alien. He slung Dotti from side to side as he tried to shake her off. His face was contorted with pain.

To Matt's astonishment, Dotti held on for dear life. She snarled through her teeth and shook her head back and forth, tearing at his arm. The alien dropped the weapon, and it clattered to the floor.

Matt scooped it up.

"Get him, Dotti!" he yelled.

With a gigantic groan, the monster backhanded Dotti with his free hand and sent the dog rolling and whining across the room, slamming against the wall.

"I'll get you for that!" Matt sobbed. Tears were streaming down his face.

But he was surrounded by Plyomith warriors, all pointing their weapons at him.

"I'm dead meat," he whispered to himself.

The Plyomith Dotti had bitten was holding his arm. "Care to do battle, *puny* one?" he snarled.

Matt looked around the room at the aliens pointing their weapons straight at him. Nothing mattered now. His parents and sisters were mindless zombies, whose bodies would be tossed out into space. The same thing would happen to him *very soon*.

He looked at Dotti, lying in the corner. She lifted her head and looked back at him, as if to say she was sorry she'd failed.

Suddenly Matt knew what he had to do.

Chapter

Adrenaline pumped through his veins. His mind barked orders.

"YEEEAAAHHH!" he screamed. "Let's do it!"

The alien looked surprised. "Well, a little bit of last-minute bravery, eh?" he said, chuckling. "Don't worry. I'll only stun you. Then we'll put you on the table and let you join the rest of your family."

Matt stuck out his hand, and another Plyomith slapped a weapon in it.

Matt took a deep breath. "On the count of three?"

The alien shrugged. "Whatever pleases you," he said sarcastically.

Nervously Matt moved his weapon from hand to

hand. His palms were sweating badly. What if he dropped it?

Taking a deep breath, he started counting. "One . . . two . . ."

Matt knew the moment had come. He prayed his plan would work as he whirled around and fired at the Bemowac!

There was a blaze of light! Geysers of sparks fountained in every direction!

He fired again, and the streaks of light on the screen faded, flared again, and finally turned a dozen different colors before going dark.

"*Baca Mooga! Baca Mooga! Baca Mooga!*" squawked the speakers hanging on the computer's sides.

WOOOOP! WOOOOP! WOOOOP! screamed the Klaxon.

Everywhere Plyomiths were dropping to their knees and slamming hands over their ears to keep out the piercing sound.

"Shrobbmgwa!" one of them shouted at Matt. He hit Matt on the side of the head, knocking him to the floor, and then ran to help the others.

All around Matt the control room was going berserk. The shutters to the window overlooking the universe were banging open and shut! The overhead lights flashed on and off! The doors to the inn flew open!

Matt frantically grabbed Ashlee and Julee by the hand and started pulling them toward the doors. Then he remembered Dotti. He looked back to see her trying to struggle to her feet. Rushing to her, he pulled her up and held on to her collar, pulling her behind him as he pushed his sisters out the door.

At the end of the hall he found his parents. They were staring in awe at the fireworks display going on in the control room.

"Mom! Dad! Run!" Matt yelled as he tried to herd his whole family toward the door. "Everybody run outside!"

His parents looked at him blankly.

"Hurry, Mom and Dad! We've got to get out of here! It's a matter of life and death!"

"Matt? Is that you?" his mother asked, as if she had recognized him for the very first time.

"Son, where have you been?" asked his dad.

Matt stared at them, remembering what Bart had said. If the Bemowac were turned off, all the information in it would flow in the other direction! That was what was happening! He had killed the source of power to the Bemowac. Now his parents' memories were coming back!

"GO! GO!" he shouted.

Outside it was snowing as hard as ever. Julee and Ashlee were already there, shivering in the cold.

"I need my coat," whined Julee.

"Me too," cried Ashlee.

"There's no time. Come on," Matt urged. He grabbed their arms and pulled them along. "If what I think is going to happen happens, you won't need them."

Matt pushed and shoved and tugged and pulled his family along through the deep snowbanks. The wind howled over their heads, but he kept them going.

Finally they reached the bend in the road. Matt stopped for an instant. He was counting on sunshine and safety being just around the corner. His mind refused to think what would happen if he were wrong.

"Just a little bit farther," he said, motioning to the others. "Come on, Dotti. Let's lead the way."

Rounding the bend, Matt gasped, and Dotti let out a yip of happiness. The sun was shining in a perfect blue sky, and rivulets of water were running and gurgling in the ditches beside the road. And best of all, the invisible wall was gone!

"What's happening?" asked his father in amazement. "I . . . I don't understand!"

"I'll explain later," said Matt. "The most important thing now is to get as far away from this place as we can."

He pushed his family on until they were exhausted. Finally they were unable to go any farther. Matt fell to his knees, gasping for air. He flopped onto his stomach, raised his head, and looked back to where Snowed Inn stood.

What he saw amazed him. "Look!" he shouted.

The chalet was quivering in the sunlight like heat waves shimmering on a summer highway. It raised slightly, and lowered again, raised and lowered, like a pulsing heart struggling with some powerful, invisible force. Then, with a mighty ZAAAAAP! the spaceship evaporated, sending a final shower of snow drops back to the spot where it had stood.

The only thing left where the inn had been was the Meyers' family van.

Chapter

Matt snuggled into the corner of the seat in the van. Dotti pushed her nose up against his leg and gave a big sigh. He reached over and patted her head.

"I can't understand it," his father said from the driver's seat. "My watch says it's late Monday afternoon. So does the radio. What happened? Have I been asleep for an entire day?"

"Calm down, dear," said Mrs. Meyers. "I'm sure it's perfectly explainable. We both probably misset our watches. That kind of thing can happen, you know. We just have to get the children back to school as quickly as possible."

Matt chuckled to himself. His parents were back to normal, all right. Still, he was glad they didn't remember any of the awful things that had happened to them inside Snowed Inn.

"What about my project at work?" Matt's father was asking impatiently. "I'm going to be way behind. And there was a meeting I was supposed to attend. Jeez!"

"Don't worry about it, Dad," piped up Matt. "There are worse things in life than missing a meeting. Right, Dotti?"

"That's easy for you to say, son," his father said. "You don't understand the important things of life yet. When you grow up, you'll learn."

Matt sank back into the seat and scratched Dotti's ear. Maybe he and Dotti didn't understand *all* the important things in life, he thought, and grinned at the back of his father's head. But there were some things the two of them did know, things they had learned at Snowed Inn. You didn't have to be the biggest to be the best. And the absolutely *most* important thing of all was your family.

Look for

BONE CHILLERS

the new TV series on
ABC this fall, Saturdays
at 10:30 A.M., Eastern
time. Check your local
listings . . .

and prepare to be
SCARED!

This collection of spine-tingling horrors will scare you silly!
Be sure not to miss any of these eerie tales.

 created by
Betsy Haynes

BEWARE THE SHOPPING MALL
Robin has heard weird things about Wonderland Mall. When she and her friends go shopping, she knows something creepy is watching. Something that's been dead for a long time.

LITTLE PET SHOP OF HORRORS
Cassie will do anything for a puppy. She'll even spend the night alone in a spooky pet shop. But Cassie doesn't know that the shop's weird owner has plans for her to stay in the pet shop . . . forever!

BACK TO SCHOOL
Fitz thinks the food at Maple Grove Middle School is totally gross. His friends love Miss Buggy's cooking, but Fitz won't eat it. Soon his friends are acting strange. And the more they eat . . . the weirder they get!

FRANKENTURKEY
Kyle and Annie want to celebrate Thanksgiving like the Pilgrims. Then they meet Frankenturkey! Frankenturkey is big. Frankenturkey is bad. And Frankenturkey may eat them for Thanksgiving.

STRANGE BREW
Tori is bored stiff. Then she finds a mysterious notebook. Each time she opens it, a new spell appears, and strange things happen. Now Tori's having fun . . . until the goofy spells turn gruesome.

TEACHER CREATURE
Everyone except Joey and Nate likes the new teacher, Mr. Batrachian–and he likes all the kids. In fact, sixth-graders are his favorite snack!

FRANKENTURKEY II
When Kyle and Annie make wishes on Frankenturkey's wishbone, they bring him back to life. And this time, he wants revenge.

WELCOME TO ALIEN INN
Matt's family stops at a roadside inn, only to find that the innkeepers are aliens eager to experiment on the first Earthlings that come their way.

ATTACK OF THE KILLER ANTS
The school picnic is crawling with ants . . . so Ryan and Alex start stepping on them. And now a giant ant wants to drag them back to its monster anthill and make them slaves.

SLIME TIME
When Jeremy sneezes, his snot suddenly takes on a life of its own–and the entire town is threatened by a tidal wave of slime.

TOILET TERROR
Tanya decides to flush her failed science project down the toilet. But her brother had just flushed their dead pet goldfish. Something strange is brewing in those pipes . . . and it's ready to come out.